THE WANDERING ADVENTURES AT HOBARTTILL

DUSTIN C. KINARD

ILLUSTRATED BY RICHARD MICHAEL GOMEZ

In loving memory of
Granny Ann and Granddad.

Together, you taught a curious and hyperactive boy
how to transform everyday life into a fun and exciting
adventure.

I will always be grateful.

CONTENTS

PROLOGUE: ONE BLANK PAGE

Flying across the Pacific Ocean in a plane unfit for a rat, Kristofer and Bianca Halladay eagerly traveled across the dark abyss. Their mission was to study an island settled far out in the water, an island recently discovered and not yet destroyed by humankind. The couple, who met on the streets of New York City as students at a prestigious university, had now traveled thousands upon thousands of miles between them.

A world traveler, that is all that Kristofer ever wanted to be. A native Samoan, he decided, on a whim, to move to America to begin his studies abroad, choosing biology as his major. Bianca, a lovely young Scottish woman at the school, majored in botany and loved finding and studying new flora. The two fell in love and married right after their degrees were complete.

Kristofer sat in his seat, madly scribbling his thoughts into his leather-bound journal, a journal that he never let out of his sight. This journal contained the very essence of who he was. He recorded every adventure, every discovery, and every thought that his mind pondered. He even practiced his artistic hand by drawing images of animals, plants, and landscapes from every inch of land that they searched.

"Le Nofoaga Lilo," the name Kristofer gave to the island they would soon reach, a Samoan translation of "the mysterious place," harbored what was thought to be a new species in the plant family. The anticipation began to build in Bianca as she looked from the window at a pitch-black canvas of night sky and the deep, dark ocean. She loved what she did, but at exciting times like this, she couldn't help but think of her only child, Malachi. He stayed home with the family's nanny as his parents circled the globe. At only eleven years old, Malachi couldn't join them yet, but Bianca couldn't wait for the day when her son would be old enough.

The pilot abruptly announced that it wasn't far now. Shaken from their dazes, Bianca brushed her long auburn hair from her face, and Kristofer looked up from his journal. They looked at each other, smiling, excited about what would come next. Kristofer pointed to the one blank page left in his journal. He would soon have to shelve this chapter and begin a new one. Kristofer slid the book into his backpack and zipped it. He looked up and smiled enthusiastically over at his wife.

The plane began to shake. Kristofer grabbed Bianca's hand. The plane was old and tended to hiccup now and then. However, this time, the commotion didn't cease. The plane shook hard, and the lights flickered as the emergency lights flashed—the plane dove straight for the ocean.

Now, it was dark and quiet, with only the groan of the ocean and the wreckage of a plane.

Chapter One

WHERE THE ROAD ENDS

An older man stood on the sidewalk, holding a sign. "*Malachi Halladay*," it said.

The man shifted his weight from one foot to the other as he impatiently waited for Malachi's arrival. He scanned the crowd as everyone exited the airport's terminal, looking at every face below five feet tall. Finally, he saw him: a young boy with shaggy dark hair. He waved his hands and the sign with Malachi's name over his head until the boy spotted him. Malachi and the flight attendant assigned to him through the unattended minors program picked up his luggage and approached the older man.

Malachi looked at him carefully. The older man was dressed smartly and seemed oddly sophisticated. As Malachi neared him, his seemingly bleak facial expression transformed, and he gave Malachi a genuine, heartfelt smile. His eyes seemed kind as if he already knew Malachi and was aware of the events of the past weeks in the boy's life.

"Malachi Halladay?" he asked, reaching out his hand to the boy. "The name's Oliver. I'm a friend of your family and your driver today. It's great to finally meet you, mate."

Malachi, too nervous and overwhelmed to say anything, gave him a large, forced grin. He shook the man's hand weakly.

"This way," said Oliver. He took the boy's bags, and they walked over to his car together.

"So, you're an American? Must be odd, the weather?" Oliver continued. "Winter to summer, innit? Right, not too hot today." The older man continued talking, but Malachi remained silent.

After helping to load all that he had into the stranger's car, Malachi climbed into the back seat. He gazed out the window as they departed from Tasmania International Airport. Everything already seemed incredibly different from his home back in New York. He noticed the air smelled like grass, and the sky seemed a different shade of blue. The sun definitely shined brighter, the plants he saw were strange, and the way the other people looked seemed odd. As the car drove down the highway, Malachi's stomach began to cringe.

"Cockney," interrupted Oliver from the front seat, breaking the silence. "That's me accent. I'm a native Londoner from the UK."

"Oh," replied Malachi, unsure of what to say.

"I'm an artist. Well, I was an artist. A grand actor!" he said, as he exaggerated his words and threw his right hand up in a Shakespearean nod. "I used to live my life in the spotlight. In the British theater, on the West End. Well, ensemble, anyway. Twice!"

Oliver turned to smile, looking back at Malachi over his shoulder.

Malachi forced a smile back.

"Anyways, got too old. I came here and never left. Now, I just drive this cab. It's a great life, you'll see. You'll love it."

Malachi stared back out of the window, and the man's voice faded into the background. He found himself in a memory from almost exactly two weeks ago.

As Malachi approached the double doors leading into the school's main office, he saw his nanny, Gwen, waiting for him. He didn't know why he had been called out of class to come to the principal's office but wasn't sure he wanted to find out. It was Christmastime, and an evergreen wreath hung upon each door, making it difficult for him to see clearly through the small windows. He stood there, partly hidden by the wreaths, watching her pace from side to side near the front desk. She stood next to the school's principal.

Gwen was a young woman who had been Malachi's nanny since he was four years old, and she was like a second mom. She was beautiful, with long red hair and fair skin. She looked much like his mother, but Gwen's red hair was brighter and fiery.

She was always a very happy, sweet presence and was extremely comforting to Malachi. Today, however, he could see the distress on her face. Malachi continued to peer in through the wreaths on the windows as he slowly pushed open the door and entered the room where she stood.

As soon as Gwen spotted Malachi, her eyes filled with tears. She quickly wiped them away and put on a gentle, compassionate smile. As Malachi made his way farther into the office, his insides trembled. Something felt wrong. Gwen walked him out to her car and drove him home, and it was there that she gave Malachi the news about his parents' plane accident.

"They're gone, Malachi," she cried, holding him against her tightly.

Oliver looked back at Malachi in the rearview mirror and saw the tears that sat in his eyes as he stared into what seemed like absent space.

"Doing alright back there?" asked Oliver, attempting small talk with the boy.

"Yeah," Malachi responded, wiping his eyes and holding on to his backpack, faking another exaggerated smile.

After a long trip from the airport, the car stopped slowly at the side of the road. Malachi looked around for a house or people, even for more roads, but all he could see were trees. He looked out of the other window, and still, nothing but plants and trees, heavy and lush, surrounded the car.

The driver exclaimed, "We've arrived, Sir."

Oliver got out and opened the car door. Malachi hesitantly stepped out onto the foreign ground. He looked around and could not comprehend how a jungle of bright green foliage could possibly be their stop, and he looked over at the driver in confusion.

"Innit a beaut?" asked Oliver as he helped the boy unload his bags from the car.

He walked over to the edge of the tree line while Malachi still stood next to the car. He could barely make out the small pathway in front of where the driver stood.

"Are we going in there?" asked Malachi hesitantly, pointing toward the path.

"Well, yes, this is the only way," chuckled Oliver.

"In the trees?" asked Malachi.

"Isn't far now. Just grab the bag, would ya?" responded Oliver.

Malachi grabbed his one remaining bag as the driver carried the others ahead of him. He ran to catch up with

Oliver, nearly tripping over the large bag as he dragged it across the remaining feet of the paved road. Together, they set off into the dense tropical forest. Malachi made each step with caution, looking down at the ground and the beaten path they both followed. He saw flowers bordering the path with colors as vibrant as the rainbow itself. There were palm trees as tall as skyscrapers above him, and he could hear the sounds of birds calling from a distance.

After following the path for a minute or two, in the shadows of the tree canopy above them, Malachi looked up to see an opening on the far end. It was very bright, and its light filtered through the forest's green. It was so bright it seemed like they were walking straight to the edge of the earth—a hole with nothing but infinite light for miles. The hard dirt path that had carried them this far slowly got softer as the dirt mixed with white sand beneath their feet. He began to feel his feet press into the earth. Like that on a beach, the soft, light sand made his shoes sink.

At the end of the path, Malachi squinted as he walked into the harsh light. And as his eyes adjusted, he was taken aback. There was nothing but white sand and a bright blue ocean ahead of him. The sound of the waves was thunderous. It was one of the most breathtaking sights he had ever seen.

"Where are we?" questioned Malachi, more confused now than before. "Why are we here?"

"This is your new home," responded Oliver. "Annie sure knows how to pick a grand front garden."

"This?! But I don't even see a house," exclaimed Malachi, looking around at the abundant natural beauty before him.

"Look over there," said Oliver, pointing to the far right.

Malachi squinted over at a small house against the tree line. They began to walk toward the house, kicking sand as they stepped. Malachi pulled the large bag behind him, leaving behind a trail that covered his footprints.

In the distance, toward the direction of the house, they could see the outline of a small person walking toward them. This person had a slight wobble as they walked and didn't stand up very tall. Their hair white and thick.

"Good day, Annie!" shouted Oliver, tilting his hat toward her.

Chapter Two

BEST SEAT IN THE HOUSE

Malachi's body was frozen.

This was the moment he had been waiting for. This was it. It was now time to reunite with Granny Annie. He combed his small, sweaty fingers through his shaggy dark hair and forced a smile onto his face.

Malachi stood, staring at her as she neared them. She had the same looks as him and his father, a native Samoan herself, with her tan sun-kissed skin. She smiled so humbly at him as he stared back with blank eyes. He found himself thinking about his parents and couldn't come to grips with the fact that this woman would now be whom he turned to for everything. She was still practically a stranger to him.

His eyes began to fill with water, and he dropped his bag on the ground. He wiped his eyes fervently, trying to disguise that he was crying, but the tears would not seem to leave. Suddenly, he felt the warm embrace of his great-grandmother, Granny Annie, as she bent down and wrapped him in her arms. This wasn't a normal hug; it was warm, strong, and loving. She kneeled before him, kindly grasped his arms, and looked into his eyes.

"It's so good to see you, Malachi! I'm so happy you're here."

Malachi nodded and smiled.

She slowly stood back up and put her hand on his head.

"And you've grown so much since I last saw you!"

He wiped away the streaming tears from his face and picked up his bag. Oliver, Malachi, and Granny Annie walked across the remaining beach toward the small house.

The pleasant smell of cooked food filled the air as they arrived at her home. Granny Annie announced that she had just finished preparing dinner and invited Oliver to stay and dine with them.

"Thank you, Annie, but I really must get on my way," said Oliver.

"Nonsense," she said, dismissing his refusal. "Have a seat and stay a while, Oliver. You're one of my oldest friends out here and always welcome to stay for dinner."

"Perhaps I can. I don't have any more cab pickups for today," expressed Oliver. "And it does smell quite nice, I must say."

When they entered the front door of Granny Annie's house, they were greeted with a tiny foyer where many pictures hung on the walls and shoes lined the baseboards along the weathered hardwood floors. In the corner of the foyer sat a scuba tank and flippers. To the left of the room was the small dining area with a sturdy wooden table surrounded by mismatched chairs facing the front windows. There was a cozy living space with an oversize couch and a coffee table with a stack of faded playing cards and dominoes.

The home was not grand in any way, quite the opposite. But it had that warm, inviting feeling of home and comfort—filled with stories and memories, well lived in and loved. But Malachi still felt the strange disconnect of entering someone else's home, cautious but intrigued.

"Malachi," said Granny Annie as she slid a chair from the dining table. "I've reserved this seat just for you. It's the best seat in the house and it now belongs to you."

Malachi sat down and looked out the window at the perfect view of the beach. It was early evening, and the sun had begun departing for the day. The sky was filled with rich shades of orange, reflecting and dancing upon the ocean's surface. He was in awe of the image before him and couldn't believe this was his new home.

"It's so beautiful," said Malachi.

"I agree," Granny Annie said, smiling at him while she placed the last pot on the table and then looked out at the sunset.

They sat at the table together and ate a large meal, nothing short of a feast. Granny Annie had prepared delicious fish and greens. There was also plenty of fruit, bread, and sauces, and everyone had a hefty portion. Granny Annie and Oliver laughed as they told stories of their adventures.

"Malachi, right down this very shore is the best fishing spot I have ever stumbled upon," said Oliver, pointing out the window toward the beach, opposite the way they had entered. "Remember all those fish we caught that day, Annie?" he asked.

"Oh yes!" she laughed.

"We ate off of those fish for weeks," said Oliver.

"There were so many!" she added as they laughed and caught up.

• • • • • • • • • •

ONCE THE FOOD WAS EATEN and the plates were clean, Oliver thanked Granny Annie for the meal. He began to leave, but not before smiling and winking at Malachi.

"It's a good life here, mate," Oliver said. "You're going to be OK."

He reached out and shook Malachi's hand.

Granny Annie got up to help Malachi with his bags and showed him to his new room. She then gave him a grand tour of the tiny home, filled with many interesting things he would want to explore in the coming days. Directly across the hallway from his new room were doors to the bathroom and a small linen closet.

"If you know what's best for you, you won't open this door!" warned Granny Annie, laughing and pointing at the linen closet. "I haven't cleaned it out in years, and the junk in there is piled high. I don't want any avalanches taking you out!" She chuckled.

All the traveling, multiple time zones, and emotions had tired Malachi, and he told Granny Annie that he needed to sleep. He walked into the new, strange room that was now his own and sat on the edge of the bed. Granny Annie checked on him like his parents used to, ensuring he was content for the night and offering extra pillows. As he got under the covers, she sat down on the side of his bed and tucked him in.

"I love you, Malachi," she said. "And I know you don't really know me, but I've loved you since you were born." She pulled the blankets up snugly around him.

"Your parents were amazing people whom I also loved dearly, and I know I can't replace them. But we will make this work, and I will be here for you always, OK?"

Malachi nodded.

"Good night, Malachi," she whispered, turning off the small lamp that lit the tiny room and pulling the door behind her as she exited.

He lay in his bed with his mind spinning. It seemed he had been with Gwen only hours earlier, back in New York City. Now, he was in Tasmania with Granny Annie and Oliver, the beach and her tiny house. He lay there, consoling himself the best he could. However, he was so tired that he quickly drifted into a deep sleep.

Chapter Three

BEEP THE CHICKEN

The morning after his arrival to Tasmania, Malachi was suddenly awakened by a sound he had never heard before. A rooster squawked a loud announcement outside his window, welcoming the morning light. Malachi jolted awake, caught off guard by the sound, nearly jumping from his nested spot on the bed.

He lay there, assessing the bedroom while untying the knot of confusion in his mind.

He remembered.

He slowly stepped out of his bed, rubbed his eyes, and ventured into the small hallway and the living room, where he squinted from the window toward the side garden. There was just enough sun to create plenty of shadows, and he could see Granny Annie holding a tin pail outside. A dozen chickens were swarming around her tall rubber boots, and he watched her sprinkle birdseed on the ground. The chickens followed her every step, devouring their early-morning breakfast.

Who gets up this early? he thought to himself, amid a large stretch and yawn.

He shuffled back to his bedroom to dig through his luggage, which he had yet to unpack, in search of a fresh pair of pants and a clean shirt. He got himself dressed and made his way outside to join her.

"Good morning!" exclaimed Granny Annie.

She watched the sleepy boy make his way over to the chicken coop. He was still rubbing his eyes, his hair stood high, and he wore no shoes.

"Come feed the chickens with me," she said. "You all might as well become friends."

Malachi liked the idea of having friends in Tasmania and thought the chickens would make as good a friend as any. Granny Annie handed him a pail of seeds, and he walked behind her, sprinkling the food out among the flock. The chicken coop was simply built—tall wooden posts stood like the cornerstones of a room, and chicken wire wrapped around them like walls. It created a large, fenced area for the chickens to run around freely while still being protected from any wild animal that may find itself nearby. All of the chickens seemed to welcome him, and he liked that he could gain their affection with a few bird seeds.

Suddenly, a large rooster charged him. Startled, Malachi dropped the pail, spilling the seeds. He ran and jumped on top of some nearby lumber, just out of the rooster's reach.

"That's Beep," said Granny Annie, laughing. "I'm thinking he must have woken up on the wrong side of the coop this morning!"

After a few moments of circling the lumber, which Malachi sat upon, Beep quickly lost interest in the boy and darted off to chase the hens in a different direction. Malachi jumped down from his roost, picked up the tin pail, now half empty, and held it in his hand. He mimicked his great-grandmother and began sprinkling some seeds on the ground before him.

"Here you go, Beep," he yelled at the rooster as he threw out the birdseed bravely. "You must be the one who woke me up this morning!"

Suddenly, Beep turned and began to run at Malachi again. The boy dropped the pail, spilling the remainder of the seeds across the yard, and sprinted for the house, never looking back.

Granny Annie stood bent over, laughing at the scene and patting her knee.

"I told you so!" she yelled after him, as she continued to laugh and as Malachi ran inside.

Granny Annie was still teasing Malachi about Beep the chicken when they sat down to eat breakfast later that morning. Malachi found that he didn't mind, though. Granny Annie's warm laugh and smile made him feel he was in on the joke. When they sat down to eat, she shared with him some of his father's adventures as a kid on the island.

"You know, when your father was a boy, he would spend many hours playing in the woods behind the house," she said. "He would run along the shores of this beach and play until the sunset." Malachi listened closely.

"He was a boy of great imagination," she continued, "making up stories of distant lands and worlds he had never seen. I knew then that he would one day travel to explore all the worlds he dreamt up."

She got up to grab a few heavy photo books, which she began to flip through, showing Malachi pictures of his dad as a boy in the very home he now lived in. Malachi vaguely remembered her bringing these books with her on a trip to New York to visit them once, a few years ago. He was much younger then and had not shown much interest.

However, this time, he looked closely at all the old pictures as they flipped through the pages. As Granny Annie turned a page, he saw an incredibly familiar photo. He had seen it before. A framed copy of this photo in his home had sat on the mantel above the fireplace. The familiar image of the white, puffy clouds and blue sky sent Malachi's mind back in time. It was right before Granny Annie had arrived in New York. It was the only time he had met her.

"She is 100 years old!" said Malachi to his father, Kristofer, as he held the framed photo in his hand.

"She's not 100," Kristofer laughed. "Maybe 80. Although, come to think of it, I actually thought she was 80 when I was your age."

"See, so now she is 100!" Malachi exclaimed.

"Well, however old she is, she definitely doesn't let it stop her from doing cool things," responded Kristofer as they both looked at the photo of Granny Annie skydiving.

The photo was so vivid and captured the colorful rainbow parachute in the background against the bright blue sky. Granny Annie's wrinkles flapped in the wind, and her eyes were wide under her goggles.

"I admire her. She is determined to live her life fully. She always has," he added, taking the photo from Malachi, looking at it, and smiling before placing it back on the fireplace mantel.

"Do you think she will like me?" asked Malachi.

"Oh, she is going to love you!" responded Kristofer. "And you better be ready for big bear hugs!"

Kristofer growled as he reached out and grabbed Malachi, tickling him as they both laughed.

"And she will like it even more if your room is clean," added Kristofer, pulling Malachi in for a squeeze.

Malachi got up, ran down the hallway toward his bedroom, stopped, and turned around.

"Does she smell like an old lady?" he shouted down the hallway to his dad, laughing.

"Just clean your room, silly," responded Kristofer, smiling and shaking his head.

His drifting mind became re-engaged by the smell of the strong floral perfume that Granny Annie wore as she sat beside him now. Hearing her speak, he realized that he had not heard anything she had said in the last few moments. She continued flipping the pages and shared the stories behind each photo as they sat together.

"Granny Annie, how old are you?" he asked.

"Ha, too old!" she responded, closing the photo book and setting it on her lap.

"I am 84 years old."

84 years old! It wasn't as old as 100, Malachi thought, but that was a lot of time and life. How many adventures had Granny Annie been on in 84 years?

Malachi took the photo book from her lap and flipped through the pages again.

Chapter Four

A BEAST IN THE FOREST

There was a knock at the door of Granny Annie's small house, which had now become Malachi's home. It had been a few weeks since Malachi arrived in Tasmania, and as he opened the front door, he was greeted by a young, athletic man. The man had long blond hair and wore a blue tank top. He carried a large backpack that towered over him, with ropes and gadgets hanging from the sides. He wore a pair of dark, sleek sunglasses on his face.

"Hey there, I'm looking for Annie," said the man in his smooth, deep voice.

At that moment, Granny Annie stepped out of her bedroom. She was dressed from head to toe in rock climbing gear, and Malachi stared back at her from the front door, perplexed.

"Malachi, are you sure you don't want to join us rock climbing today?" asked Granny Annie as she sat down to tie her boots.

Malachi gave a nervous laugh and quickly declined the offer. He knew what he wanted to do today, and it wasn't climbing up rocks. But picturing his elderly guardian partaking in such an activity was humorous yet impressive to him.

"OK, just stay close to home," she said. "I'll be back before sundown."

When Granny Annie had finished tying her last boot, she and her friend left for the cliffs not far down the shore. Malachi quickly slipped on his shoes and exited the back door, adventuring to the edge of the trees behind the house. He had been dreaming of making a clubhouse for a while now, someplace special in the Tasmian jungle that was just his, and wanted to see what secret places he could find in the woods.

The underbrush was very thick, making it hard to move around in the dense foliage. Briars, tall weeds, and large vines covered each trail he attempted to blaze. He used a small pocketknife from the kitchen drawer to create a clearing. Sawing through the vines and briars, Malachi marked the path with broken branches so he could easily find his way back to the house. He had learned this trick when his parents had taken him hiking in the mountains.

Skinks and insects were everywhere, scurrying across his path with each step he took. He also spotted a giant and colorful butterfly, the largest he had ever seen. The trees were bright, and the briars were thick. He had to stop to carefully untangle his shoes and pants from the dangerous plants many times.

Malachi briefly wondered if Granny Annie considered this part of the jungle "close to home," but he decided the adventure was worth the risk. And besides, she was busy rock climbing.

Eventually, the newly discovered path led him straight to a narrow stream that seemed to flow for miles in both directions. He removed his shoes and socks and stepped into the flowing water. It was cool and refreshing. Malachi took a deep breath before jumping completely into the cold water. The forest was beautiful, and he sat in the stream looking at all the beauty around him. He saw a blue-tongued lizard sunbathing on a rock along the shore and what seemed to be a perfect clearing for his new clubhouse directly behind it. There was a huge tree with a giant trunk and massive branches, giving the space plenty of cover and shelter.

He stood out of the water and walked to the bank's edge. He was dripping wet and pushed his hair back out of his face. After picking up his shoes, which lay next to the sunbathing lizard, he wandered over to the big tree.

He began clearing some of the plants out of his way, pulling them up by their roots, throwing dirt around, which stuck to his wet skin and clothes. He used the pocketknife to cut away the remaining weeds and brush that littered the space, and he used the edge of his shoe to rake out the dirt. He found a log a few feet away and rolled it over, deciding it would be perfect for his new chair, as well as a smaller one for a footrest. He sat on the organic furniture for a moment and wished he wasn't alone. He wished he had help. He wished he had a friend to play with.

He was shaken from his daydream when something moved among the green bunch of dense ferns. He stopped in his tracks and held his knife out in front of him, waiting for whatever it was to make its next move. After a moment, he dismissed it as just another lizard and returned to clearing away the brush. He was much more cautious this time. When he was sure that whatever had been in the bushes had now left, a large dark shadow lept from the ferns and ran extremely fast over and behind the large tree.

Malachi jumped back, dropping his knife and falling to the ground, where he sat still, frozen, with eyes wide open. He had no idea what had just escaped from the plants, and whatever it was had moved so quickly that he saw nothing of it but a quick, furry blur. He nervously stood up and picked up the knife. He tiptoed over to the large tree, following the tracks imprinted in the dirt, holding out the knife and trying to swallow his fear. He stretched out his neck to try to see around the giant tree without getting too close. He could see the outline of the beast crouching behind one of the large tree roots.

Malachi's breath caught in his chest.

"Hello," he whispered, crouching a few feet from the tree, trying not to scare the beast.

He glared into the dark shadow and saw two eyes glaring back at him. Malachi put his hands in front of him, dropping the knife in a friendly gesture. After a moment of intense adrenaline and complete silence, the eyes in the shadow began moving closer. Malachi took a deep breath as his heart began to pound loudly. He stepped back a few steps as the beast made its way closer to him. Malachi got ready to jump up and run, now second-guessing his decision to stay. The beast stepped one step closer, out of the shadows, revealing itself in a light-filled spot glistening through the tree canopy above.

Relieved, Malachi smiled.

The "beast" was much smaller than he had anticipated and way less intimidating. Standing before him was a small, beady-eyed, furry animal—a young Tasmanian devil. She peered at Malachi and slowly took steps closer, one after the other, pausing to sniff the air at each stop. Her tiny nose bounced around in the air as her lips curved upward. She made her way over to him, and he reached out his hand to her. The animal was hesitant but seemed approachable.

"Hey there," he whispered kindly, patiently waiting for the animal to approach him.

It finally got close enough again that Malachi could reach it. He slowly brushed the top of her head with his fingertips as she stepped closer, and his fingers ran down her back.

"You're really nice," whispered Malachi, trying not to scare her away.

He gently petted the top of her head as the animal warmed up to him, now brushing his leg with a slow wag of her little tail. He giggled as she tickled his hand with her pink tongue. After a few moments of them cautiously getting to know each other, he stood up and took a step. The Tasmanian devil pounced at his shoe, and when he took another, she again leaped at him. He began scooting backward with tiny steps, and each time, the furry animal would pounce on his shoe, biting at his shoestrings.

Malachi laughed and took off running, and she began to chase him, which turned into a full-fledged game of chase. He grabbed a stick, throwing it as far as possible. Despite her short body and legs, she took off for it at a very speedy pace. She retrieved the stick and returned it, dropping it at his feet. He again threw the stick. And again.

They played until they were both worn out, then collapsed on the ground of the newly built clubhouse as the orange of the sunset began glowing throughout the forest.

As the little Tasmanian devil jumped on him and licked at his cheeks, Malachi was sure he had found a new friend.

"Is this your home?" asked Malachi. "Here in my clubhouse?"

His new friend looked up at him with eyes full of confirmation.

"Do you have a family? Do you have a name?" he asked, knowing she probably didn't.

He looked over his shoulder, back toward the ferns where he had found her.

"How about Fern?" he asked as he began to pet the Tasmanian devil.

"I think that name fits you well," he said, looking at her and nodding, confirming his decision.

The orange sky was getting darker, and Malachi knew Granny Annie would return from her adventure soon. And, she would be looking for him.

"Fern, it's getting dark, and Granny Annie will be worried if I don't go back home soon," he said. "I'll be sure to come and visit you tomorrow and the day after that and the day after that. We will be best friends, for sure."

As he got up and walked away, Fern began to make a noise, and Malachi turned around and looked back. She stood there, looking at him, and he realized she would be left alone in the forest, which was now darkening with the sunset. He walked back over and bent down in front of her.

"It's OK. I'll be back in the morning, really early," he said. "I promise."

Malachi touched her head and got up to walk away.

Fern began to whimper.

"Well, I can't stay here all night," he exclaimed, with shrugged shoulders, looking back at her for an answer. "And I don't know what Granny Annie will think of me bringing you back to the house."

He paused a moment, now thinking over the situation. He knew exactly how it felt to be alone.

"I guess you can come home with me," he said hesitantly, "but you'll have to stay outside."

Fern, in excitement, took off and ran to catch up with Malachi, running circles around his feet. Together, they returned to Granny Annie's house along the path he had made earlier that day. They stopped at the back steps, and Malachi ran inside. The boy hesitantly opened the door of the small hallway closet, the same closet Granny Annie had warned him of. He winced as he tried his hardest to keep the junk from spilling into the hallway, fumbling around in search of the stacked linens, and eventually pulled out an armload of blankets for Fern. He exited the back door, bringing them out to her, and made a bed under the back steps. He lovingly tucked her in for the night.

"Sleep well. I'll see you in the morning," whispered Malachi. "And try to stay quiet. We can't let Granny Annie know you're here." Fern nuzzled into her bed, happy to have a home, if only for the night.

Malachi ran inside the house, and Granny Annie was standing in the living room, having just arrived home. She held herself up against the wall as she reached down to untie each of her climbing boots. She looked up at Malachi as he entered the room.

"Malachi, I was beginning to wonder when you would come home. Did you have fun? Would you like something for dinner?" asked Granny Annie, peering at him over the top of her glasses while she removed the boots from her feet.

"No thanks, I'm not hungry," he said, grabbing an apple from a bowl in the kitchen and quickly running to his room, nervous that Granny Annie might sense something was up.

He tucked himself into the bed and took a few bites of the apple. He was excited to spend the next day playing with his new friend, but more than that, he was excited just to have a friend. He lay down with a smile and turned out the lamp.

• • • • • • • • • • • •

THE FOLLOWING DAY, Malachi was awakened again to the sound of the rooster, Beep, welcoming daylight to the coop. It had become a custom each morning and no longer frightened Malachi as much. Remembering Fern, he ran out of the back door barefooted. He crouched down and looked under the steps to find the animal, with no luck. His heart began to race as he searched all around the steps. He looked high and low, trying to think of anywhere she may be.

Did she leave? he thought, surprised at how sad the thought made him.

He began to run toward the garden, scoping it out, when he caught eyes with Granny Annie over at the chickens. She waved him over from a distance and called his name. Malachi slowly moved toward her, his eyes scanning the area with every step, looking both high and low.

Once he got over to where Granny Annie stood, he spotted Fern. She was having a friendly game of tag with a few chickens, although the chickens didn't seem to be having as much fun as she was.

"Look what made its way into the garden this morning!" exclaimed Granny Annie, pointing at Fern. "These creatures are not usually too fond of humans, naturally shy. This one, however, came right over to me this morning."

Malachi took a cautious step toward the coop.

"Isn't she adorable?" questioned Granny Annie as she reached down to pet her.

Fern then spotted Malachi and ran over to him, jumping as she circled him excitedly. He couldn't lie.

"Her name is Fern," said Malachi. "I found her yesterday when I was in the forest. She followed me home, and I made a bed for her beneath the back steps. That's why she's here. But I had to! She doesn't have a family or a home."

"Well, why didn't you tell me?" asked Granny Annie.

"I didn't really know what you would think of her," said Malachi.

"I think she is absolutely splendid! I'd love to have her as a guest here at the house!" she exclaimed in an animated voice.

"Really?!" said Malachi, barely able to contain his excitement.

"Of course," Granny Annie laughed. "A friend of yours is a friend of mine."

Malachi was relieved and excited about her decision. He thanked Granny Annie again and again. That night, Malachi made Fern a better bed, this time in his bedroom, right next to his.

• • • • • • • • • •

ALTHOUGH THE TRAGEDY of his parents' death never left his mind, with each day, it got easier. Malachi began to develop a great new home and family in Tasmania, which helped to fill the void left in his heart.

Oliver began visiting for dinner regularly, often checking on Granny Annie and Malachi. He gave Malachi and

Fern free rides around the neighboring towns and helped Malachi construct his clubhouse in the forest. As an actor, Oliver was very good at dreaming up new worlds of make believe. He would become a pirate, an alien, or Malachi's favorite: his uncanny portrayal of the Queen of England.

In the evenings, Malachi and Granny Annie would sit down to share their lives' stories together. She often came home with stories of mountain-climbing expeditions, sky-diving, and skiing adventures. She amazed Malachi that she could do all these things, being as old as she was. He remembered the photo of her skydiving that had sat in his family's living room as a child. In return, Malachi would recount the moments of his day.

Tasmania had begun to feel like home.

Chapter Five

THE MYSTERIOUS PACKAGE

One morning, about a month after Malachi had arrived in Tasmania, the postman arrived at the door of the small home. He carried with him a package.

"Good morning!" yelled Granny Annie from the chicken coop as she waved her hand toward him.

"Good morning!" said the postman, waving the parcel in the air. "I have a package for a Malachi Halladay."

"That's me!" shouted Malachi from the chicken coop, brushing his hands on his pants as he ran over to greet the postman.

Malachi took the package from the man, thanked him, and ran inside with it. He couldn't imagine who would send him a package, and the suspense excited him. Maybe it was from New York? Perhaps a surprise from Gwen?

He shook the small box but heard nothing. He looked at the front of the box, and there was no sender's name, only an address, one he had never heard of. He went to the drawer in the kitchen in search of something to open the parcel with. After no luck and having harbored his excitement for long enough, he settled on a fork and used it to tear the tape away from the box.

He pulled out layers of paper stuffing, and for a moment, it crossed his mind that the box may be empty. He dug down into the crumpled paper that stuffed the box and neared the bottom. With one more piece of packaging removed, he saw, at the very bottom of the box, a weathered, leather-bound book. Malachi quickly recognized it. The outside of the book looked more worn than the last time he had laid his eyes on it.

Granny Annie had now made her way to the house and stood at the door watching him. She stepped inside, and Malachi turned toward her quickly with bewilderment in his eyes.

"It's my father's journal," he stuttered.

Granny Annie walked over to the boy and the box and picked up the letter that sat next to the book.

She unfolded it and began to read it to herself.

"The letter says they found it on the plane," she said. "It was one of the only things they found that could be salvaged—stuffed inside a waterproof backpack."

Granny Annie put her hand on Malachi's shoulder. He just stood there, examining the outside of the book, having not taken his eyes off it as she spoke. Afraid to open it, unsure that he was ready to unpack what he had pushed down for weeks, Malachi picked it up and embraced what remained of his father. He ran to his room, jumped on his bed, and stared at the book that he laid beside him. He vividly remembered his father sitting at their dinner table in New York City late at night, reading over the book and scribbling all his records inside. He had never been allowed to touch the book before and felt a bit odd now having the book in his possession.

It sat there, just staring back at him, and his curiosity began to wander, thinking about what lived among the many pages of such a well-traveled journal. What would he find? All of his father's work was here. His entire life was recorded on these pages. What if there were things he didn't want to find out? The fear began to subside as greater curiosity kicked in. His imagination swarmed with all of the many possibilities.

He grabbed the book and cautiously opened it to the first page, where he found his father's signature and a photo taped to the page. It was of his parents on one of their many adventures. Bundled in fur in what looked like subzero temperatures, Kristofer and Bianca Halladay were wrapped in fluffy fur coats. Their cheeks were bright red, greatly contrasting with the white hills in the background. It seemed there was nothing but white fluff for miles.

"Where could this have been taken?" Malachi thought as he brought the book closer to his face for better examination.

Even though it seemed to be freezing in the photo, as he looked closer at his parents' expressions, it was as if their love for one another and the burning excitement inside them kept them happy and warm.

Malachi slowly closed the book. He wasn't ready to go any further. He set it on his nightstand. In time, he may skim the pages more in depth, but the freshness of his parents' death was still too real. He was overwhelmed with emotions and he knew he was unprepared to face the book head-on.

Fern came into the room and lay down on the floor next to the bed where Malachi sat. He looked down at her, touching her gently with his foot. He then looked back over at his bedside table. There was a chocolate wrapper, his lamp, and his father's journal. He, more than anything, wanted to be just like his parents. He missed them and thought about them constantly. He wondered what they would think of his new home, awesome new clubhouse, and pal Fern. He had heard them talk about their adventures with such excitement for so many years and was always jealous and wanted to join.

He got up from his bed and walked to the kitchen where Granny Annie was preparing a meal.

"Can I help?" asked Malachi.

"Of course you can," said Granny Annie. "I can always use a pair of extra hands. You can dice these potatoes."

Malachi was willing to do anything, anything, to get his mind off of his parents and the book. His day had already been so overwhelming that he only wanted a distraction. Granny Annie looked over at Malachi and smiled. She knew how he was feeling and slid over the tomatoes.

"You can dice these, too."

Chapter Six

THE TOWERING IRON GATE

By now, there had become a distinct path to follow through the woods from the house to the clubhouse. Malachi had even taken the time to construct makeshift bridges and walkways along the pathways with Oliver's help. The clubhouse was now a standing structure, also thanks to Oliver, who had helped Malachi build a few walls and a floor.

A dark blue sheet with yellow stars hung as a door. Inside, Malachi had collected an odd array of furnishings, from his tree stump furniture to Granny Annie's old garden bench. Malachi was always searching for new furniture and decorations, and the eclectic collection added a rustic comfort to the place. He loved collecting things both from the forest and from other places.

Today, Malachi was determined to find something new, something to use as a new table, so he and Fern no longer had to sit on the floor during their lunches. Together, they crossed over the stream and began their hunt. Fern sniffed the earth below as Malachi looked far for anything that may seem usable. They had searched this area many times and cleared it of anything new or useful. He, instead, decided to take a new path this time, veering from the beaten and established trail.

The new trail took the two of them deeper into the woods, farther than ever before. Malachi broke branches and made markings, like he always did, to ensure they would not get lost as they made their way along the unknown and untraveled trail. Fern stopped and sniffed many interesting logs along the way.

Malachi's stomach began to growl and he dug into his backpack to find the two packed sandwiches Granny Annie had made that morning. He looked around for a place to rest and eat and spotted a clearing ahead. Fern was also hungry and spotted the ideal picnic area. She ran ahead of the boy, and Malachi ran after her. The luscious forest around them began to thin and open up as they neared it. They walked out into the bright open field, where the tree line ended, and they stopped. Malachi gazed in awe as he shoved the sandwiches back into the backpack.

Before them, at the far right side of the field, stood a very large and very old house, unkempt and overgrown with spidery flowered vines and tall weeds. The cleared area of the estate's garden was huge and included a lush stream. A wooden waterwheel stood next to a few wooden sheds littered among the stream's edge. Surrounding the complete estate, cutting it off from Malachi and Fern, was an enormous iron gate.

From the looks of it, it had been many years since anyone had visited the estate. Nothing looked freshly used or groomed. Fern and Malachi walked up to the tall iron gate, peering inside as it towered over them. They walked along the outside of it as Malachi thumped his hand along the large iron bars. He was filled with curiosity and now wanted to find a way to explore inside.

Malachi was too small to climb over the tall iron gate but much too large to go beneath it. He stood and pondered, sticking his foot between two iron bars and pushing himself up. He got a good foothold, but with the next move, he slid back down. He turned to Fern to see what she thought, but when he turned to her, he realized she was no longer standing at his side. He spun himself in a complete circle, looking all around. He looked as far as he could to the left and the right.

Panic erupted in his heart as he began looking around for his friend. He ran along the gate, calling her name loudly, cupping his hands to his face, projecting his voice.

"Fern!" he yelled. "Here, Fern, come here, girl!"

He ran the length of the gate and, in an instant, happened to run right past her. As soon as his mind realized what he had done, he took a few steps back. Standing in front of him was Fern, looking up at him, wagging her tail, and standing on the opposite side of the gate. He stood, baffled.

"How did you get in there?!" he questioned her.

Fern stared at him, panting, and glanced to her left. Malachi looked away from where he stood and noticed an opening in the gate. He spotted a high iron arch above the entryway and an iron gate door that appeared to be rusted open. Beautiful flowers grew on the vines that ran up the arch and covered most of the crafted ironwork. Now, standing directly in front of the entrance, Malachi looked up and read the words molded into the archway.

"Hobart Mill," he read aloud.

He hesitated as he watched a skink run up the fully bloomed vine that ran up the large iron door. He stepped over the threshold onto the estate grounds, and Fern ran up to meet him.

Malachi expected to feel excited about exploring the mill, but instead, he suddenly felt a chill. He began to feel very odd and glanced down to Fern for comfort. All of a sudden, he heard what now seemed to be music playing. Fern heard it, too. She tilted her head sideways and listened.

"Where could that music be coming from, way out here?" whispered Malachi.

He cocked his head and listened intently, trying to determine the direction from which the music was coming. It seemed to be resonating from down the stream a bit, from one of the old wooden grain sheds that lined the water's edge. But they all looked abandoned, just like the rest of the gardens and the large house.

Malachi decided to move boldly toward the grain shed to see if that was where the music was coming from. With every step, his heart leaped increasingly inside his chest. Fern followed closely behind him. She stopped and growled as they got closer, but Malachi patted her head, reassuring her that it was all right.

The music got louder and louder, and Malachi found himself only a few feet away from the shed. The music was very clear and sounded like a live performance. Voices sang out peculiar notes and sounds. However, when he took one more careful step forward, the music ceased to play.

"It stopped," he whispered, looking down at Fern. "It must know we're here."

Malachi's heart began to race.

He turned and walked away, skipping into a slight run, while he looked back over his shoulder constantly. Nothing, however, presented itself.

He paused.

He felt the need to escape and not be seen. However, he also fought himself against the thought. Sure, there was terror, but there was also the adrenaline of discovery, the allure of not knowing. This was his adventure. Malachi turned around and took steps back toward the shed.

He took another step forward and another.

With each step he took, he felt more and more courageous. Every adventurer needed to be bold. The door to the shed was only inches away from him now. With hesitation and timidity, he reached out and grabbed the rusted door handle.

The door creaked loudly as he pulled it open. Fern ran inside as soon as the opening was big enough for her little body to fit through.

"Hold on!" he shouted in a whisper.

Fern, however, was already inside. Malachi, taking a deep breath, quickly entered the shed right behind her.

The room was quiet. It was packed full of old burlap grain bags, hay bales, and a heavy layer of dust. The room was dark, full of shadows, and Malachi's eyes slowly had to adjust to the dark. Once he could fully make out what lay ahead of him, through squinted eyes, he saw nothing but a messy, unoccupied room.

But where had the noises he heard come from? he thought.

Fern whimpered, and Malachi looked down at her with shrugged shoulders.

"I don't know, girl. There is nothing here."

After a long day of fun and mystery, the sun had begun to set. It was time for them both to return home. They left the shed and walked across the mill lawn, but Malachi was still confused by what had occurred. They approached the large iron gate, and as they exited through the archway and rusted open doors, Malachi continued to look over his shoulder. He glanced back occasionally, searching for any sign of an answer. The thoughts and questions now swarmed through his mind. He was determined to return and explore. He wanted to find more.

There was a mystery there. Malachi was sure of it.

"We will come back tomorrow," he told Fern.

They trekked the long way back, through the forest, across the stream, and past the clubhouse toward home.

Chapter Seven

MCCARTHY'S ANTIQUES AND ODDITIES

Tomorrow was not the day to return to the mysterious mill. Instead, Malachi had to go shopping with Granny Annie and Oliver.

"But I don't really want to go," exclaimed Malachi, ready to return to the mill as soon as possible.

"But you always enjoy going into town," said Granny Annie.

"I know. I just have a lot to get done at the clubhouse," said Malachi.

"Well, it'll be there later. You'll have plenty of time to work on it. You might even find something in town you want to get for it," responded Granny Annie.

"OK," he responded, disappointed that he wouldn't be able to return to the mill until the next day.

"We'll have fun!" said Granny Annie. "We always do!"

The ride into town was long, but Oliver filled it with conversation, as always. Malachi sat restless in the back seat, and just as he was sure he could not endure the confined seat any longer, Oliver pulled into a space and parked the car. They had reached the center of town. Malachi flung the car door open and jumped out.

Oliver opened the car door for Granny Annie as she slowly stepped out, collecting her empty shopping baskets. Malachi and Fern stretched while they waited. Granny Annie began to wobble toward the grocery store, which was an easy walking distance from the prime parking spot. The central hub of the town was small, and sidewalks connected all of the local shops. The old brick stores stood in line, one next to the other, with tall ceilings, wooden beams, and bright open storefronts. Oliver took Malachi to neat shops while Granny Annie bought groceries.

They walked along the sidewalk, looking into each shop as they passed. There were shops filled with jarred fruits and preserves, appliances, and candles; a mattress store; and a bookstore. And, as they neared the end of the block, Malachi stopped.

"McCarthy's Antiques and Oddities," he read aloud.

It was written in bold, thick gold lettering across the large window. Wide wooden blinds were pulled down inside.

Malachi squinted to peer between the slivers of the blinds as he put his face, cupped between his hands, to the window.

"I can probably find some awesome things for my club-house in there!" exclaimed Malachi.

"I'm sure of it," responded Oliver.

Oliver removed his flat cap and held open the door for the boy.

They entered the dark, dusty store with the chime of a bronze bell that hung tied to the doorknob. The smell inside was musty. Tiny dust particles floated through the air, illuminated by the lines of light that shone through the slats of the blinds in the storefront windows.

A man coughed at the back of the store and cleared his throat.

"Yes, welcome," grunted the shopkeeper as he walked from the rear, perhaps McCarthy himself.

"Thank you," nodded Oliver.

They navigated the items that overcrowded the aisles and searched through the piles of old pots, vintage metal signs, and antique high chairs. Oliver spotted an antique typewriter, which he showed to Malachi. Malachi had never seen the machine before and stared in amazement as Oliver demonstrated the machine's ingenuity. Fern sniffed at a teapot set sitting on the ground, and Malachi tried his luck at riding an old bicycle. Unfortunately, the rust and clumped cobwebs had already stopped the pedals from rotating.

There was a sack of old marbles and a few shooters that Malachi found.

"These are cool!" Malachi said, looking at Oliver.

"Agreed," he responded. "It'll be quite the purchase!"

Malachi carried the sack with him as they continued through the store.

There was an entire section of taxidermied animals: a wombat, a few possums, and bats floating in jars of liquid. He spotted tiny porcelain fairies, marionettes that hung from the ceiling, and boxes of clown dolls. A print of the extinct Tasmanian tiger (or Tasmanian wolf, depending) was on the wall in a beautiful, gold ornate frame. It had a dog-like head, a mouth ajar with sharp teeth, the stripes of a tiger down its back, and a kangaroo-like tail.

"What a weird-looking animal," said Malachi.

"Unfortunate that it's gone forever," responded Oliver.

As Malachi turned his gaze from the print, he caught eyes with the shopkeeper, who was watching them at the end of the aisle. Feeling awkward, Malachi quickly looked away.

"Help with anything?" asked the shopkeeper.

"I reckon this sack of marbles will be it for today," responded Oliver, looking for confirmation from Malachi.

Malachi nodded.

"That's it then," said Oliver, smiling, as they walked to the pay counter.

Malachi put the sack of marbles on the counter, and the shopkeeper bagged them as Oliver handed him cash.

"Thank you," said Malachi as he reached out to grab the bag from the man.

As he did and began to pull it away, the man held tight to the bag. Malachi looked up at him, again catching eyes. An uneasy vibe washed over Malachi, but the shopkeeper smiled and let go.

Near the exit door of the shop, sitting in the front corner of the room, was an old wooden crate. The crate stood in place of a table with a floral print cloth draped across it and a collection of creepy china dolls on top. Malachi stared at the bottom of the crate, which was still raw and exposed below the cloth. Falling to his knees, he crawled over to it and pulled back the drape, exposing the naked, unfinished wood. He uncovered the remainder of the text that had initially caught his eye from the aisle.

"Hobart Mill," he read.

Malachi remembered seeing these words only the evening before. The exact words were welded into the iron archway at the mill that he had spent the last day exploring. He shuffled across the floor, circling the crate, searching the other sides for more words—for any more information. But only those two words were stamped in a bold, thick font.

Oliver, intrigued by what he saw happening, decided to chime in.

"Malachi, have you found something?" he asked curiously.

"Oh, it's nothing, just this old crate. I thought I could use it, but I've decided against it," Malachi said as he stood up and tried to move along, dusting off his pants, not wanting to raise any suspicions from the older man. If Oliver were to find out and mention anything about the old abandoned mill to Granny Annie, she might find it unsafe and not want him to return.

"It's an old mill crate," said Oliver, still focused on the item the boy had shown interest in.

"Those used to be all over town, back when the Hobart family still produced all of the flour for the townspeople," he explained. "However, that was quite a while ago. There's nothing too special about that crate now other than it makes a nice china doll table." Oliver chuckled.

"Why did they stop?" asked Malachi, whose interest was now piqued again by Oliver's knowledge of the situation.

"I'm not really sure. Not sure that anyone really knows," answered Oliver. "One day, the shipments just stopped coming into town, and no one ever heard of the Hobart family after that."

"Well, isn't that kinda strange?" asked Malachi.

"Yeah, I guess it is," responded Oliver. "It has been many years since then, but from what I can remember, the family was always quiet. They stood out among the other people in town. Didn't know 'em much. I, myself, was new to the area back then."

Malachi noticed that the shopkeeper had left the counter and had moved closer to where they stood. Oliver caught Malachi's gaze over his shoulder, realizing he had been speaking loudly.

The shopkeeper began to whisper. "Honestly, between you and me, I think they were hiding something, scared to associate with the townspeople who might discover their secret," he said.

Oliver turned and stepped aside so Malachi had a clear view of the man.

"They say that Crimson Hobart, the husband and father of the family, went crazy, and his family ended up leaving after he was taken to a hospital and moved up north. They were never heard of again."

"Really?" said Oliver to the shopkeeper.

"In fact," the shopkeeper added, "no one ever really knew where the mill was located for all those years. It was kept a big secret. The crates would just kind of show up in town every morning. That mill is somewhere nearby, but nobody I know has ever been able to locate it. At least that I'm aware of."

Malachi's heart was now racing.

Malachi knew exactly where that mill was. He knew that if he ever said anything about it, there was a chance he may never get to return to it. Perhaps they would think it was unsafe for him to be there. His curiosity peaked, and he was antsy to discover the mystery of the mill and the strange music he had heard the day before. He stayed quiet to avoid ruining his possible adventure and chose his words carefully. This discovery excited him more than anything before. He couldn't risk messing it up.

"Very interesting. Thank you," stated Malachi bluntly, dismissing the conversation as he hurried them out the door.

The shopkeeper followed behind them, and Malachi watched him standing at the doorway as they walked away from the shop.

Oliver then took them to visit a few more shops that day, and other than an ice cream cone and a sack of marbles, they found nothing interesting to bring back home. Oliver, Malachi, and Fern met Granny Annie and helped her load up the car with brown grocery bags and her baskets filled with fruit. They traveled back home.

Once they arrived home, and after several trips from the car to the house, the groceries were all unloaded, and Oliver left them for the day. Malachi knew he didn't have enough time to make the trip to the mill before sunset, and he decided to help Granny Annie prepare dinner. He washed the vegetables and stirred the pot, but in his mind, his imagination was a whirl of possibilities. There were so many questions that filled his mind:

Where did the Hobart family go?

Why was the mill such a secret?

And most of all, where did the mysterious music he had heard the day before come from?

He knew he had to go back and find out.

After dinner, Malachi sat on his bed, Fern curled up beside him, and took out his father's journal. He opened it to the first page again. That was as far as he had ever gone in the book. He stared at the picture of his parents as he had before: the snowy background and their happy smiles. He could see the happiness in his parents' eyes, the joys of life, adventure, and love.

He stared at the picture for a while, nervously tapping the book with his fingertips. He nibbled at his lip, a nervous habit, as he tried to work himself up to go further this time. He took a deep breath, and with it, he turned to the next page for the first time, and his eyes began to water. Moments later, he closed it, throwing it to the other side of the bed. He quickly turned off the lamp on his nightstand, and as he lay down, wrapping himself in the blankets on the bed, he began to cry.

Fern navigated herself over the lumpy blanket that covered him and found a spot to cuddle in real close. She nuzzled herself against him, and he held her for comfort. The wet spot on his pillow got darker with every tear. He cried until he fell asleep.

Chapter Eight
THE MARBLE GAME

The following day, Malachi and Fern headed off through the woods. On his back, Malachi carried his heavy backpack full of sandwiches, drinks, a flashlight, and even his new marble set he had gotten in town the day before. They made their way past the clubhouse, across the stream, down the path, and again found themselves standing at the entrance of Hobart Mill. Malachi darted inside the gate and ran across the garden toward the shed. He quickly and boldly swung open the door. But, there was nothing but a silent, dark room. Malachi looked down at Fern and shook his head.

"Empty," he said. "I guess we'll just have to stay and wait."

Malachi and Fern sat down on the floor in the dark room. He was determined and decided to sit and wait until he found something or until something found him. Fern sniffed the hay as Malachi played with the marbles in the center of the floor. The sun barely lit the room, which shone in through the small, dusty, stained windowpanes. Malachi sat on the floor of the shed humming songs and playing fetch with Fern, but after what seemed like many hours, he felt restless and got up to stretch.

He stood there and looked around the dark room. It had begun to rain outside, and he could hear the steady beating of the drops on the shed's roof. Nothing exciting had occurred the entire time they had been there, and no sounds other than his own footsteps and raindrops could be heard. He packed everything into his backpack, tightened it onto his back, and walked toward the shed door.

He stood at the door, disappointed, as he held it open for Fern, who slowly followed behind him. He allowed her to exit first and took one last look around before closing the door behind him. The rain beat down on top of them, and his shoulders sank as he dragged his feet across the wet grass. He had waited and waited to get back here, but all of his waiting and excitement had been in vain. He knew he had heard something a couple days before. He was sure of it.

Or was he? Malachi started to doubt himself.

"Let's go," he said to Fern.

Fern followed behind him as he moped his way across the lawn. They walked along the stream, and Malachi kicked a rock that splashed into the water. The rock made a large ripple in the water, surrounded by the many tiny droplets made by the falling rain. He could hear the frogs croaking down the stream and Fern jumping through the high, wet grass beside him.

He stopped.

"Shh," he whispered as Fern sat down beside him and cocked her head to the side, looking up at the boy.

Fern's ears perked, and Malachi looked down at her quickly. They both now heard something. It was something new, something different than the rain and the frogs. He turned to look behind him, realizing the noise had come from the shed they had spent the entire day in. He looked back down at Fern, not moving and listening closely as the raindrops slid down his forehead and dripped from the tip of his nose. It was a loud noise that they had heard. Something had moved inside.

Malachi turned slowly and began to tiptoe back across the wet lawn toward the shed door. He slowly opened it as it creaked and stared inside at the dark, cluttered room. At first, it looked just like they had left it, dusty and abandoned. However, upon closer inspection, he noticed one of his large shooter marbles sitting in the middle of the floor. Malachi was sure he had collected them all when he left.

He cautiously entered the doorway of the shed, slowly creeping his way across the old wooden floor. He looked into the shadows as he moved toward the marble. Behind him, his wet shoes left prints on the dirty, creaky planks. He nervously bent down to pick up the marble. While leaning over and looking down at it, his eyes on the floor, he heard another sound, a noise similar to the one he had heard before.

Thump.

This time, the noise he heard was much louder and much closer to him. It sounded like something had just fallen from the ceiling rafters to the hard wooden floor before him. His heart raced as he stared down at the floor, afraid to look up. Fern growled as she backed away from his side, and his hand trembled. Something was standing before him, and he could feel its presence.

Malachi slowly stood up with the marble in his hand, peering forward into the dark room. Ahead of him, at the very back of the shed, stood an upright figure. It was outlined only by its shadow. It stood about as tall as Malachi, maybe a few inches shorter. It was hard to tell. Startled, Malachi threw the marble straight into the darkness, directly at the shadow. It landed short, hitting the dirt and rolling toward the figure. Malachi watched as the shadow bent down, grabbed the marble from the floor, and threw it back toward him.

It was a gentle throw. The marble hit the floor with a "thud" and rolled until it hit the tip of Malachi's shoe. The shadow moved one step closer. Malachi softly kicked the marble with his foot and rolled it back into the room's shadows. Once again, it was returned to him by the dark figure. This back-and-forth continued, and with each return, a step closer, the mysterious figure would come.

Malachi was frozen in place. As the shadowed figure slowly approached him, one step at a time, Malachi gulped and gazed ahead of him. He shivered, but he couldn't move away. Fern stood near the doorway, peering into the room. Her back hair stood up as she continued to growl, her growls getting louder. The shadowed figure took one more step closer, and with that step, it exposed itself in the light of the small window near the door.

This figure was unlike anything Malachi had met before.

Large, bulging eyes in a light pea-green-colored face stared back at him. Two dark black pupils were directly set on Malachi, one slightly smaller than the other. The eyes were somewhat crossed. Its mouth sat slightly ajar, panting like a puppy, with a single jagged white tooth off-centered near the front of its bottom lip. It was clearly not human and stood upright on its back legs, a clumsy slumber in its stance.

The rest of its body was covered in dark teal fur, except for a black fuzzy goatee that jutted from its chin and a black furry stripe upon the top of its head like a mohawk. It had small green hands and feet, just like its face, which were much less hairy than the rest of its body. It was like that of a fairy tale creature that Malachi had seen and read about in books of make believe.

Malachi stood inert in the center of the room. He was nervous and anxious; his hands were clammy, but what he didn't feel was terror. He looked back into the eyes of the creature. Its large eyes looked back at him, and Malachi sensed that it meant him no harm. It simply stood there, patiently waiting for a continuation of the marble game that they had begun. It slowly bent down and reached out its small green hand to roll the marble toward Malachi.

Suddenly, a voice rang out from the rafters above.

"It can see you. Hide yourself!" said the voice, shouting out from the shadows of the shed.

Malachi was immediately surrounded by scrambling and grunting noises as the creature that had stood before him disappeared. The voice he heard was a high, feminine-sounding voice. Malachi spun around, peering into the dark, looking for the voice's owner. He squinted his eyes and scanned the depths of the room for both the creature he had seen and the mysterious voice.

"It's OK. I won't hurt you!" exclaimed Malachi from the center of the room, shouting into the darkness.

However, whatever had been there before was now gone. Fern was circling the room, sniffing and still growling.

"Hello?"

Malachi stood for a moment longer in silence, but nothing happened. He turned around toward the doorway, thinking he might give up. At that moment, the small marble from the rafters above dropped in front of him. He reached down to pick it up, and upon standing back upright, the creature from before was again standing before him, panting and eager to continue to play. Malachi smiled at him and was surprised when he received a slight smile in return.

"I'm Malachi," he said.

The creature attempted to return the greeting and nodded in a mumbled grunt that Malachi couldn't quite understand.

"Don't let it see you!" yelled the distant voice again. It sounded closer this time—however, the creature standing before Malachi ignored the warning and didn't run away like before.

"Don't make me come down there!" yelled the high voice, echoing out again from the dark shadows of the room.

The small creature didn't move at all. It stared straight at Malachi, gave a friendly grunt, and patiently waited to play the marble game.

Then, there was another loud noise.

Thump.

It was the sound of something substantial hitting the wooden floor as if it had also fallen from the ceiling rafters.

The dust in the room was stirred up, the tiny particles floating around in the sunlight that beamed through the window. Up from behind Malachi walked a similar creature, frightening him as it emerged from the darkness into the light.

This new creature wore blended shades of purple fur, very different from the teal creature standing before him. This new one also seemed more evolved than the previous one and was female presenting instead. It had shades of purple fur upon its head and a light lavender face. Its face resembled that of a bird's; however, it had no wings, nor did it have a distinguished beak. Its nose was large and bulbous. It stood just about as tall as the other one, and it walked right up to the other, grabbed its arm, and pulled, turning as if to guide it away back into the shadows along with it.

"Come on, Zeke!" urged the purple one, pulling at him with all her strength.

It was the same voice that had resonated throughout the shed earlier. Somehow, Malachi could understand this one perfectly when it spoke, unlike the grunts made by the other. She continued to pull on the one called "Zeke" but couldn't get him to budge.

"Excuse us a moment," she said to Malachi, lifting her hand to him as she turned and began whispering toward the teal creature, trying to coax it into following her away.

While they continued their spat, another noise resounded out of the dark.

Thump.

"We get to play?!" asked another voice from behind Malachi.

This new voice was also feminine but raspy and excited. Malachi turned around and again saw another one of the small furry creatures coming up from behind him. This new one's fur was patterned with stripes of many colors, including yellow, green, and blue. She was similar to the purple one, but her face was a soft, citrus orange, she wore a giant smile on her face, and her eyes beamed with excitement. She was bright and full of life, and the fur upon her head bounced as she walked. "How's it going? I'm Jeri!" said the colorful creature to Malachi, giving a quick wave as it approached him.

She also stood about a foot lower than the boy.

"No, no, no!" fussed the purple one, dragging Zeke behind her. She walked up to the colorful creature and continued in hushed tones.

"We cannot associate with this thing!" urged the purple creature, aggressively pointing its small lavender finger toward Malachi. "We must go now!"

"Rai, look at it!" said the colorful creature, pointing at Malachi. "He looks nice and fun, and I want to play...and so does Zeke, isn't that right?"

She looked over at Zeke, and he agreed in a fit of groans and mumbles.

All the while, Fern sat crouched in the corner, unaware of how to react to the new creatures.

"Do you not realize what this is?" demanded the purple one to the others. "This is a human. We cannot be seen by humans, much less play with humans. We must go; it has already seen enough," she said, gesturing at Malachi, who watched them in bewilderment, amazement, and total confusion.

"This is a human?" questioned the colorful creature, who had given the name Jeri. "It's too short to be a human! And it doesn't even look mean." She turned to Malachi.

"What are you?" asked Jeri.

"Um...I'm a boy," he responded hesitantly.

"See Rai, it's a boy, not a human," said Jeri, directing her statement toward the purple creature.

"Well, I am a human," said Malachi. "A human boy."

"So are you or are you not a human?" Jeri asked him briskly, with a baffled face and large hand gestures.

"I am a human," said Malachi.

"Really? No kidding?" responded Jeri in a high voice, now looking closely and sniffing at the boy. "Well, it's decided. I still like him," she said to the purple one.

"You can't be friends with a human, Jeri," the purple one, Rai, responded.

"I can be your friend," said Malachi to Jeri. "I can be friends with all of you. What's so wrong with being a human anyways?"

"Humans are the reason we've been locked in this shed for so long," responded a defensive Rai, waving her hands around in the air. "Crimson Hobart warned us about them, you, before he left. He told us to stay in the shed, and we would be safe, that no one would find us here."

"Crimson Hobart?"

Malachi remembered Oliver mentioning the Hobart family the day before while they were in town. The Hobart family, or at least Crimson Hobart, had known of these creatures' existence.

Was this the secret they were trying to keep? he thought. *Is this why no one knew of the mill's location?*

While Malachi lost himself in his deep thoughts, the creatures disappeared from the room, and it became quiet. When he suddenly noticed that they had left, shaking himself from his daze, he looked around and called out their names, "Rai! Zeke! Jeri!" but found nothing. He jumped atop crates and hay bales, looking behind them and using them to climb upward. He hung from the rafters and stood on his tiptoes to search for the creatures.

After intently seeking them out to no avail, he picked up Fern from the corner where she still sat, and together, they walked through the dark, quiet room toward the exit.

The closer they got to the door, the more Malachi's confusion grew as he noticed the spot where the door had been was no longer there. He felt along the wall, starting to panic. The doorway had seemed to have disappeared. He took a quick glance around the room. He beat at the wall where the entrance should have been, kicking it. He turned around, peered into the center of the room, and noticed the single marble still lying there. He took a few steps toward it, and Fern sniffed the air.

They walked, side by side, deeper into the dark wooden shed toward the marble. Fern whimpered, and at the same time, Malachi also noticed a shift in his surroundings. The temperature in the shed rose substantially all of a sudden. The air felt drier, and he squinted to see through the dark shadows of the room. In the near distance, where the dark back wall stood, there was a sound. He squinted more, bending his body forward and staring, cocking his head to listen closely.

The faint sound he heard grew louder until it became a mighty roar. A loud, pounding force sounded like it was coming straight toward him. He turned around, looking back at where the doorway once stood, and began to move backward. The walls around him began to break and crash down, and Malachi quickly closed his eyes as a bright light filled the cracks until the dark room was illuminated entirely with a blinding white light.

Chapter Nine

MOUNTAINS THAT MOVE

Malachi and Fern stood paralyzed as he forced his eyes to adjust to the blinding white light that seemed to pass through his tightly closed eyelids. He peered down at the ground as he forced his eyes to open, one at a time. He looked at his shoes, which sunk into white sand beneath them. He lifted his head, squinting and using his hand as a visor, and looked out ahead. Before them was the blinding reflection of the sun, dancing among the bright blue surface of the ocean.

It was quiet, except for the roar of the waves that crashed, blurring the line separating water from the sky. The water resembled thousands of clear sapphire diamonds, poured out and glimmering by the sun's light. For as far as he could see, there was nothing but an array of tropical, luscious colors and the smell of saltwater air.

Fern moved closer to Malachi, practically sitting upon his foot. He looked down at her, trying to muster up expressions of comfort for her, all the while filled with perplexity himself. She dug at the sand beneath her and growled.

Malachi walked to the water's edge and bent down to wet his hand in the shallow tide. The water was cool compared to the heat of the direct sunlight atop a blanket of gleaming white sand. He still couldn't completely open his eyes, and as he continued to squint, he looked far down the shore at nothing. The sweat beaded on his forehead, and he wiped his brow with the ocean water. He got up and turned, looking back at the beach and the dunes. He needed shelter from the sun and walked toward the shade of the trees lining the beachfront. A familiar voice rang out from the sky as he approached the tree line.

"Look out below!"

A large, fresh coconut dropped at Malachi's feet onto the sand. He quickly glanced up, covering his face to shield his eyes from the sun. Above him, swinging from the branches of a very tall palm tree, were streaks of yellow, green, and blue.

"That was close!" shouted Jeri as she hopped down the long, narrow trunk of the high palm to the hot sand where Malachi stood.

"These coconuts are likely to knock you out! You might want to keep a heads-up!" said Jeri, smiling and winking as she approached the boy and reached down, grabbing the fruit from the shore, which lay next to the boy's feet.

Jeri stood a bit shorter than Malachi, looking up at him. Her colorful fur glinted in the sun, and her eyes were bright with wonder. Her smile was wide and cheery. He watched her as she picked and peeled at the coconut, walking over to a leafy plant where she sat down with it beneath the plant's shade.

The shed was long gone, and Malachi had yet to learn where he was. What had been the mill, with its grand lawn and garden and tall iron gate, was now blinding sand and coconut trees. There was a vast ocean on one side of them and deep, tropical flora on the other. It was eerily quiet, other than the sounds of nature surrounding them: the ocean waves, the wind, the birds, and the animals.

A rumble in the bushes behind startled them, and Jeri hopped over to examine the edge of the tree line. She moved almost chimp-like, jumping as she stepped, and less like a human. Malachi watched her and followed slowly as Fern took her stance, growling at the unknown. Jeri grabbed a stick and poked into the forest, moving over branches to get a better look into the heavy, dark shadows.

"Yah! Yah!" she shouted, poking the stick into the plants.

She stepped closer, poking further, and out of the green leafy wall ahead of her came a loud grunt.

"OW!"

The grunt was followed by a tumbling Zeke, all tangled in vines, with a mouthful of leaves. The creature rolled out and landed on his back, with his feet up in the air, crossed, and tumbled above his head. The sand beneath him spread and covered his fur. His teal fur was much brighter in the sun than in the shed's shadows.

Jeri stood over him, eyes wide, and then fell down on her belly laughing at Zeke. Malachi also laughed and ran over to help his new friend untangle from his predicament.

"Where are we?" Malachi asked Jeri while he continued to help Zeke by unraveling vines from his fur.

"I'm not actually sure," she said excitedly. "It sure is a lot of fun though, isn't it?"

"So you don't know why the mill turned into a beach? I turned to leave after you all disappeared, and the next thing I knew, coconuts were flying toward my head!" he exclaimed.

"I don't know the answer to that either," said Jeri. "We have never been outside of the mill before! It's so exciting!"

"Well, how are we supposed to get back?" he questioned out loud, although he was sure that Jeri had no answer.

Malachi began to think. It was still early in the day, but he knew if he did not somehow make it home before the evening's sunset, Granny Annie would be worried and searching for him. He looked around, trying to uncover clues as to where they may be or how far away from home they had come.

Maybe we're on the beach close to Granny Annie's house? he thought. *Perhaps home isn't that far away.* He consoled himself with that thought.

"Hey, aren't there three of you?" Malachi asked. "Where is the other one?"

Another large, fresh green coconut fell from a tall palm, landing only a foot from Malachi. He stopped and looked up, staring at the tall palms again. Above him, he saw a figure with purple fur clinging to a tree.

"Help!" yelled Rai, high up in the tree.

"Hey guys!" Malachi yelled over to Jeri and Zeke. "Rai is in the tree up there, and I think she may be stuck."

"She's not stuck!" chuckled Jeri, dismissing Malachi's worry. "It's not THAT high."

"Help me down!" Rai yelled more aggressively in response to Jeri's comment.

"Oh, well, maybe she is stuck!" responded Jeri, still smiling. "Just swing down! It's fun!"

"I can't just swing down, Jeri!" yelled an annoyed and afraid Rai. "It's very high up here!"

"OK, OK, I'm coming up," shouted Jeri.

At that, Jeri ran over and jumped onto the tree. She wrapped her little legs around the trunk and easily climbed to the top. She remained up in the tree for a moment, talking Rai through untangling herself from the vines. She then helped Rai back down the tree and to the ground safely.

"Much better!" said Rai, brushing herself off. "It's decided. I do not like heights!"

"How did you get up there, anyway?" asked Malachi.

"Well, I climbed up there," she said, very matter-of-factly. "I was lost and was hoping I could spot the mill from up there."

"Did you see anything?" asked an eager Malachi.

"Nothing, just more trees," Rai replied. "It doesn't look like we're anywhere close to where we were."

"So how did we get here?" he asked.

"I was going to ask you the same question, Mr. Human," she responded abruptly, pointing her finger at Malachi. "This did not happen until you arrived."

"It's definitely not my fault!" he replied. "This hasn't ever happened to me either."

"We've been in that shed for as long as I can remember," responded Rai, pacing back and forth, "and whatever this is that's happening, well, it has never happened before you.

I don't even like the beach. There's too much sand in my fur!"

Rai brushed the sand off of her.

"How is this even possible?" questioned Malachi, kicking at a fallen palm branch in the sand.

"Hey, you all, look over there!" yelled Jeri, who had climbed back up a palm.

She pointed out toward the distant sky.

"I can see mountains! Maybe if we head that way, we can climb high enough to see which direction home is."

"That's a great idea," responded Rai to Jeri. "Though it doesn't seem like we have many choices. Let's go."

Zeke responded with an agreeing grunt as he sat in the sand near Fern, trying to pet her as she slowly moved away each time he crawled closer. She glared at him from the corner of her eye and growled.

"I can lead the way," said Malachi. "I can use my knife to cut a path."

"Oh no!" responded Rai, almost immediately. "You've already done enough! We can't trust humans, and we shouldn't even be talking to you. We'll be on our way; we've got it from here."

"What makes you think you can't trust humans?" asked Malachi, defensively placing his hands on his hips and watching the creatures turn and start for the overgrown jungle.

"We're not bad!" he shouted.

"Crimson Hobart warned us," responded Rai, turning to look at the boy, "and he kept us in that shed, protecting us and guarding us from your kind."

She pointed straight at Malachi.

"I promise I won't hurt you," he responded. "I want to help you."

Zeke's stomach growled loudly, and he placed his hands on his belly and turned red, giving everyone a nervous, one-toothed smile as they turned to look at him.

"Let's go," said Rai to the other two who stood there, watching her.

"Wait!" shouted Malachi, thinking of the packed lunch in his backpack. "I brought enough snacks to share."

"He has snacks! The boy has snacks!" cheered an animated Jeri, holding her stomach. "Let him come with us, pleeease!"

Rai realized that she, too, was beginning to get hungry. She looked at her friends, the jungle, and the beach and questioned where their next meal would come from. She thought for a moment.

"Fine," she said. "You can come with us."

"But this doesn't mean we are friends, and I'm going to keep my eye on you!" she added.

"Aggh!" groaned Zeke as he ran up and grabbed Malachi, happy his new friend would join them.

The group collected themselves and set off through the crowded bush at the beach's edge toward the distant mountain. It was darker underneath the crowded treetops, and they cautiously made each step atop crumpled leaves and underbrush. Jeri led the way, still pushing over plants with her stick. Zeke followed clumsily behind the group, and in his arms, he carried a bunch of fresh coconuts he had taken from the shore.

As they got deeper into the wooded area, the underbrush began to clear, and the soft, sandy ground began to harden. Malachi turned around, at a glance, to check on Zeke, who fumbled behind him along the path. With each step, Zeke tried to balance the many coconuts that hindered his view of the path before him. Malachi turned and saw Zeke peeking between the stacked fruit as he made each fumbled footstep, and before Malachi could warn him, Zeke tripped on an exposed root. He fell forward, and all the coconuts flew from his arms onto the path ahead. He quickly stood up and brushed himself off as the group stopped to wait on him, all alarmed by the noise and commotion of the fall. Zeke mumbled in frustration as he gathered the scattered fruit, trying to pick them up and fit them back in his arms.

"Hey Zeke, don't worry about those," said Malachi encouragingly. "Look up. There are coconuts everywhere. There's no need to bring your own!"

Zeke stopped and looked up at the canopy of green that surrounded and covered them. Malachi was right. Palm trees bearing coconut fruit were everywhere. Zeke laughed as he dropped the fruit he had already collected. He slapped himself on the forehead, amused by his own ignorance, and ran to catch up with the rest of the group.

"And...we're off!" shouted Jeri as she pointed forward and continued to journey deeper into the forest.

Zeke started to hobble and grunt as they pushed forward with each step. His toe was still sore from tripping over the root. Malachi noticed that he was having a hard time walking, and he stopped. He removed his backpack, bent down, and let Zeke crawl up on his back for a piggyback ride. He handed his backpack, still full of sandwiches and grapes, over to Rai, who reluctantly took it from him. As Malachi had, she tried to wear it on her back, but the backpack was a little large for the creature. With a few adjustments to the straps by Malachi, they made due, and she walked through the forest with the straps from the backpack dragging behind her.

As they walked, Malachi heard a light patting sound that beat in rhythm. It continued as they walked along, and he noticed it was coming from Jeri, who was patting her belly as she made each step. Rai began to hum in unison, and Zeke started to make little beats with his mouth as he clung to the boy's back. Jeri then began to sing. The music was beautiful, and Malachi realized it was similar to the music he had heard coming from the shed at the mill. These little creatures made the music that had mystified him the past days.

They continued as they walked along, unaware of Malachi's sudden interest. The music was peaceful and caused the boy to fall into a slight trance as his worries and concerns seemed to leave him. He felt happy and content, and life seemed to be amazing. He smiled and bobbed his head to the beat. These creatures were so mysterious and odd. However, they created such a beautiful and magical sound.

They walked for quite a while, crawling over large boulders and through slick mud while singing songs in a native tongue unfamiliar to Malachi. With a loud groan, Rai finally stopped, flung the backpack off her, and sat on the ground.

"I'm tired," she exclaimed, "and this bag is heavy!"

"I agree," said Malachi, dropping Zeke down from his back, worn out from having carried the creature for so long.

"This actually seems like a great place for a rest," said Jeri, pointing toward a nice clearing in the trees ahead.

The group settled down on the grass, and Malachi, sitting in the circle with them, opened his backpack to share his meal. He passed out the sandwiches and fruit; they ate as they sat and rested.

"Thanks for carrying Zeke," said Jeri to Malachi. "It's a very nice thing to do, especially when you're a scary human boy." Jeri looked over at Rai and giggled.

Rai huffed and turned her body away from the group.

"She's nice, too," said Jeri to Malachi. "Sometimes."

"So, what are you?" asked the boy curiously.

"A Bogo," responded Jeri. "We're all Bogos."

"And what is that?" he asked. "Where are you from? And where did you learn to sing like that?"

Jeri opened her mouth to say something, but before she could answer any of his questions, a scream interrupted their conversation.

"Ahh!" screamed Rai, jumping up and running over to Jeri as she squealed and ran in circles, fervently brushing off her hair in dramatic chaos.

"It's a frog," she yelled, pointing over at where she had sat with her lunch. Fern growled loudly and sniffed the air.

While they had been resting, a bright orange tree frog had decided to join the camp, jumping and landing on a branch near Rai. Zeke chuckled, rolled, and then chased after the frog, who was busy jumping away quickly, fearing for its own life. Fern's tail wagged as she followed behind. Jeri looked over at Malachi, both laughing.

"I don't like heights, and I don't like frogs," said a breathless Rai, still squirming and brushing her hands off. "I'm ready to go home!"

Jeri looked around and jumped over to a tree nearby.

"I'll climb this tree and see where we are," said Jeri, stretching against the tree and scratching her back among the bark. "We should be getting close to the mountain."

She jumped up and climbed the tree. This tree stood higher than most other trees in the area, which gave her a great clear view. She reached the top and looked out across the vast forest again. She used her hand as a visor from the sun and squinted as she peered toward the direction of the mountain. She looked right, left, and then turned around, gathering a panoramic view of the beautiful landscape.

"Ummm," she murmured, putting her palm to her cheek. "This isn't good."

Her heart began to race.

"What do you see?" shouted Rai.

"It seems the mountain is gone," shouted Jeri, perplexed.

The group below stood in a circle, looking up in bewilderment at Jeri. She crawled back down to join them.

"What do you mean it's gone?" questioned Rai.

"How could a mountain disappear?" asked Malachi.

"Should we continue to go forward?" asked Rai. "How will we ever find out where we are?"

"Too many questions!" shouted Jeri, throwing her hands up in the air.

"What did you see up there, Jeri?" asked Malachi.

"Nothing but the treetops!" she responded. "There was nothing else in sight. And if we can't get any higher, I don't think we will ever figure out which way is home."

At that, Zeke let out an exasperated groan and dramatically fell to the ground, with his arms and legs stretched out around him.

"Ohh!" he grunted.

Fern ran and jumped on the furry creature, licking his face as he laughed and gave her a pet. The others slowly sat down, one by one, and looked at one another, unsure of their next steps or how they would find their way back home.

"This is not good," sighed Rai.

"We'll figure it out," responded a hopeful Malachi.

"And, Human, how will we figure it out exactly?" she questioned him. Malachi was just as nervous as Rai, but something deep inside him told him to be brave.

"I'm not sure yet," Malachi responded, "but we will."

Chapter Ten

A SECRET YELLOW BOOK

Malachi and the group gathered the garbage from their picnic together and journeyed aimlessly through the forest, headed toward where the mountain had once stood. They continued to question how a mountain could just move. Malachi knew the only hope of finding his way home would have been to climb that mountain. Now that it was gone, he wondered how he would return. The sun was slowly departing beyond the horizon, and he was sure Granny Annie had begun worrying about him at this hour. His chest fluttered, and the fear inside of him announced itself. However, Malachi was also driven by the excitement of the journey so far.

A cluster of trees made their ceiling for the night, and the forest became darker and more mysterious. The sky turned deep shades of orange as the sun embraced its last few moments, the trees only a silhouette against the dusk sky. Birds flew into their nests among the trees for the night and rested together, protecting their homes and one another from the unknown. The frogs croaked, the bugs swarmed loudly, and creatures of the deep exhaled bellied groans throughout the forest.

Each group member was anxious for dawn and knew they wouldn't get much sleep that night. Jeri and Zeke climbed up a tree and nestled among its branches. Rai found an encave in the bottom of a tree trunk, and Malachi and Fern sat together against that tree, peering out into the darkness, determined not to sleep but instead to keep watch over camp all night long. Fern cuddled up against Malachi, nuzzling beneath his arm as she let out a small whimper.

"It's OK, girl," he said, patting and holding her for comfort. "Just a few hours. We can do this."

Zeke began a loud, constant snore, frightening Malachi until he looked up and realized the origin of the snarly growls. He saw his friend hanging from a limb, sleeping peacefully. Malachi smiled and chuckled to himself. He patted Fern, who was growling quietly at the sound of the snoring creature.

Suddenly, Malachi heard another noise come up from behind him. It was the sound of rustling leaves on the ground. Fern growled louder, snarling her lip, and he grabbed at the flashlight he had taken from his backpack.

He fumbled with the switch until, finally, he flicked the light on just in time. In front of him, he saw an upright living outline standing over him. He was frightened until he spotted the rainbow colors that painted Jeri's fur.

"Sorry if I scared you!" she whispered, sitting on the ground next to Malachi, who still held Fern tightly.

"Just a little," he said, breathing quickly. "What's wrong? Can't sleep?"

"Not really. Zeke snores so loud!" she said, laughing.

"Yeah, I don't know how he can sleep so well out here. It's creepy," he responded.

"I don't think he worries much," said Jeri. "He's a very carefree guy."

"I've noticed!" said Malachi.

"I realized you never got an answer to your question earlier, that one about who we are," she added. "I wanted to share this with you." She handed him a little yellow book.

"Rai probably wouldn't want me to show you this, so I was waiting for her to go to sleep," she said, giggling.

Malachi held the small yellow book in his hands. His hand rubbed across it, feeling the engraved cover. There was a foreign script that he could not read and a picture of a royal galloping horse decorated with rings and jewels in the center. He lifted the book to his face and could smell the leather. The smell reminded him of his father's leather-bound journal.

"What is it?" he asked.

"I have had this book forever. For as long as I can remember, it has been with me," said Jeri. "It seemed completely useless, filled with a bunch of blank pages. What good is a book without words? Well, that was until you arrived today."

Malachi squinted and cocked his head as he stared at her, not sure he was understanding completely.

"It somehow has changed. Look," Jeri said, gesturing toward the book.

Malachi opened it and flipped through the many blank pages, all bare except for the very first one.

"It must mean something," said Jeri, "but I can't read it."

Malachi looked down at the book's single scripted page.

"Can you read it to me?" she asked.

Malachi shined his flashlight at the book as he started to read.

IN THE BEGINNING

IT BEGAN WHEN THE KEEPER OF LIGHT, UNBOUND BY TIME OR SPACE, TOOK THE FORM OF A NEPALI SADHVI, A VIRTUOUS WOMAN OF THE HINDU FAITH. IN THIS FORM, THE KEEPER OF LIGHT EXPLORED THE MOUNTAIN RANGE IN SEARCH OF THE INFAMOUS YETI. THE YETI WAS THE DEFINITION OF EVIL AND DAN-

GER. *Its massive size, ability to camouflage with the surrounding snow-capped mountains, and evil temperament brought sheer horror to the mention of his name. Many people thought the Yeti was just folklore, but it didn't stop manipulators and villains from using the story to intimidate others and make them afraid to venture out alone.*

When the Sadhvi discovered the creature, it captured her and took her to its cave, where seven other Yetis also resided. She was thrown to the floor, scratched and bruised, as the mammoth creatures towered over her and planned out for her an unfortunate fate. Unbeknownst to them, and before they could attack, the Sadhvi mobilized her magical powers and cursed all eight Yetis with a spell of goodness, brightness, and humility. The size of the giants dissipated as a sign of humbling, their snow-white fur changed to many colors of the light spectrum, and their evil hearts became good.

The Keeper of Light gave the Yetis a new name derived from their native language: Yetah. This new name, "Bogo," meaning "Bearer of Goodwill," would describe their new life's purpose. The Keeper of Light dispersed the Bo-

GOS ALL OVER THE EARTH. THEIR SOLE RESPONSIBIL-
ITY BECAME FIGHTING DARKNESS AND BRIGHTENING
THE LIVES OF HUMANITY. THEY WOULD FIGHT FOR
PEACE, COMPASSION, AND ACCEPTANCE OF DIVERSI-
TY.

ONCE CREATURES OF DEATH AND VIOLENCE, BOGOS
BECAME IMMORTAL. WHEN A BOGO ACCOMPLISHED
ITS DESTINY, OR FAILED TO DO SO, IT WAS THEN GIV-
EN A NEW LIFE THROUGH REINCARNATION. THIS NEW
LIFE CAME WITH NEW CHALLENGES AND A NEW PUR-
POSE TO FULFILL.

NOW CREATURES OF LOVE AND BRIGHTNESS, BOGOS
WOULD FOREVER REPEAT THIS CYCLE TO SEEK AND
FIGHT FOR HOPE AMONG HUMANITY.

Jeri and Malachi both sat still for a moment as he finished reading the page.

"Wow, those are big words," responded Jeri, eyes wide
open.

"So you were once evil?" asked Malachi.

"Well, it seems so," she responded with a nervous laugh.
"At least that's how we started."

"But you seem so nice," he added.

"I guess we have the Sadhvi to thank for that," she responded. "The Keeper of Light guides us now!"

"Wow, that's kinda scary," said Malachi.

Jeri laughed nervously.

"So, then, how did you arrive at Hobart Mill?" he asked.

"No idea," responded Jeri. "I guess we were reincarnated from our ancestors when they had completed their purpose. The mill is where our lives began. It's where we were sent. It's really all we know."

"But nothing's there," responded Malachi. "It's abandoned. What purpose could you have in a grain shed?"

"I guess only The Keeper of Light knows why we are there. We've also been waiting to find that out. I assume our purpose will become known one day, and until then, we just wait in that musty grain shed."

"So you didn't know about this?" he asked her, pointing at the page in the book.

"Not until today," she responded. "Not until you arrived, Malachi."

"Whoa," he whispered.

"Maybe it's a sign," she said in a spooky tone while twinkling her fingers in front of her. Malachi smiled, but part of him wondered if Jeri was right. If the Bogos were supposed to be there, was he supposed to be there, too?

Jeri took the closed yellow book back into her tiny hands, tucking it away in her fur as she turned to climb back up the tree to her resting spot.

"I'm just going to put this away. Lots to think about," she said. "And remember: don't tell Rai! She's funny about this kind of stuff." Jeri laughed while she rolled her eyes.

"Let's chat more about this later. I'm exhausted!" She yawned, nuzzling into her branch.

Malachi sat there, wide awake, thinking about the book that Jeri had shared with him.

What in the world are these creatures? he thought. *What a funny name, "Bogos." And they used to be Yetis? Those are abominable snowmen, right?*

"I'm not sure what's happening, Fern," he whispered out loud to the Tasmanian devil curled up beside him.

His mind raced to exhaustion as he found himself conflicted about keeping a good watch over the camp or, instead, not looking too deeply into the darkness, afraid of what he might see. He hugged Fern and himself in a form of comfort for his restlessness.

Malachi sat there, anxious. Had he just seen a set of eyes in the darkness peering back at him, or was his mind playing tricks? He quietly began humming. He hummed for a while until he realized what he had been doing and immediately stopped, afraid to bring attention to himself because of the noise.

He sat there, completely hushed in the dark forest, trying to remember where he knew the song from. He began to hum it again, lower this time, still keeping watch over the night. He felt an ease pass over him as he continued to cuddle next to Fern and hum to himself. It was familiar, and it was sweet.

He smiled.

He remembered.

It was a song his mom once sang to him, her lullaby she had written just for him when he was a baby. She would sing the song while tucking him into bed at night, an often incomplete song, as he would fall asleep before the ending. Tears now welled in his eyes. He, almost silently now, hummed as his eyes began to flutter. Each time he blinked, he drifted, and soon, he was fast asleep against the tree with Fern in his lap.

The wild forest groaned as the hours of darkness and the slithering of the night beasts passed them by. They each slept soundly.

Chapter Eleven

GARDEN OF THE SLEEPING GIANT

As the sun dawned, it shone its beams through the canopy of treetops above where Malachi and the Bogos camped. The small sunrays warmed the forest as the sun stood tall in the morning sky. High in the tree branches, Zeke snuggled closer into the crook where he slept.

A sudden shake of the ground beneath them, however, awaked Rai. She opened her eyes quickly, dazed and confused, as she glanced around at the inside of the musty, hollow tree where she lay. Another shake followed almost immediately, and she screamed. The scream caused Malachi to jump up from his post where he had sat all night, leaning against that very tree. Wiping his eyes and dropping Fern from his arms, he stood up and peeked over at Rai.

The ground shook again, and Malachi stumbled backward over a root. Zeke fell from the tree, shaken from his bed, and landed safely in a lush bush beside Malachi. Jeri awoke and jumped down from her tree perch.

"What was that?" she exclaimed.

The intense shake happened repeatedly, with a loud boom that resonated throughout the forest. The sound got noticeably louder as the ground shook more aggressively. With a final loud boom, a huge shadow was cast over the campsite. The light from the sun was washed away as if night had again fallen upon them. Slowly, each journey member turned around and peered upward at where the sun once shone.

Before them all stood a huge, dark shadow that was dense and impenetrable. As it neared them, they could see that it was, in fact, a very, very large man. It was a giant man whose massive, dirty feet stood eye level with them and whose upper body easily cleared the tops of the trees.

They ran and dove into the tree cave where Rai had slept that night. They all squeezed in as tight as they could around her, arms and legs left outside, wiggling well within the giant's gaze.

"What...What are you doing? What is it?" Rai screamed.

"Shh," whispered Malachi.

They all stayed quiet and still.

The giant reached down and grabbed the tree, pulling it right out of the ground. The roots came out of the earth with it, and he tossed it like a branch over his shoulder out into the vast forest behind him. They all tumbled out about the grass, still trying to huddle together. They were now completely vulnerable before the giant.

The ground shook again, this time like no other time before. It bounced them high into the air as their huddle fell apart, and they toppled back down on the dirty, grassy terrain. The giant had taken a seat, now sitting beside them, clearing out every tree that once stood in the spot his large bottom now claimed. He looked down at them with large squinted eyes. His forehead was frilled with wrinkles as he examined them. His face's stern and curious expression changed as the sun-wrinkled skin on his face molded into a dimpled smile. His dark, suntanned oak complexion contrasted greatly with his bright grin.

He had large, bushy brown eyebrows filled with sprouts of green leaves and twigs. They sat atop his large, tired brown eyes. His hair was shaggy and draped across his forehead and the tops of his enormous ears. Strands of sun-bleached green, like meadow grass, mingled throughout the tree trunk brown and the stone gray roots of his hair. His skin was dirty, and his muted brown clothes were baggy and stained. He wore no shoes, and his toenails were unclipped and jagged. His large hands lay instead like boulders on the ground at the ends of his stocky arms.

"Bula!" he yelled, as he grinned and spread his arms out wide in a welcoming gesture as if to encapsulate the entire surrounding land.

"Welcome to The Garden of the Sleeping Giant, me friends!"

His bold and powerful voice resounded amongst the surrounding tree trunks and echoed about the forest. It was a slow, gravelly voice, and he spoke in a way Malachi had never heard before. Was this how all giants talked?

He and the Bogos looked at each other, stunned by the giant's smile and welcoming greeting. They each got up, brushing themselves off and laughing nervously toward one another, heads down, as if not to catch eyes with the giant and admit that they might have been wrong to be afraid.

"Me name is Mesee Nausori, and me will be your guide today throughout your tour of the gardens. Tickets, please!"

"Um, tickets?" said Malachi with a nervous laugh.

"Yes, of course! For me tour! Are we all here? Is there anyone we are waiting on?" asked Mesee.

"Sorry, um, giant sir. We don't have tickets. We don't even know where we are," responded Malachi.

"No tour?!" Mesee questioned, surprised and sounding somewhat disappointed. "Hmm...then how did you get here? You are pretty deep in the jungle. Are you lost? I have never seen you before."

"Ac-actually, we are kinda lost," said Malachi, now squinting through the early-morning sun to gaze up at the giant and stuttering to find his voice. "We are not sure how we even got here, to the jungle of the giant's garden," he stuttered. "Do you think that you can help us?"

"The Garden of the Sleeping Giant," Mesee corrected him, laughing with a deep roll of his belly. "And, of course me can! Where do you need to go?"

"We just want to get back to where we came from, if you don't mind," Jeri said.

"Where's this place you come from?" he asked, and then, smacking his forehead in an apologetic and absent-minded gesture, he added, "And, friends, what are you names?"

"It's a pleasure to meet you, Mesee," said Malachi, reaching out to prompt a friendly handshake and quickly retracting the motion, realizing that the giant's hand was too large to shake and would surely crush his.

"Um, my name is Malachi," he said, pointing to himself and then to the others, "and this is Zeke, Rai, Jeri, and Fern."

"We're looking for Hobart Mill," Rai impatiently interrupted. "If you could just point us in the right direction, we'll be on our way."

"This place you say does not sound too familiar to Mesee," he said, scratching his head in thought, "but me help you search for it!"

And with that, and no warning at all, Mesee reached down with his two giant hands and scooped up the group. He then stood up and took a huge step. He carried them in his palms as they began to travel through the forest again, hovering high above the treetops. Malachi was amazed as he looked out from the palm of the giant at the beauty that surrounded him. He held on to Fern, and they enjoyed their ride and the rare view courtesy of Mesee.

Rai sat in Mesee's left outspread palm, along with Zeke. She held tight to the giant's large ring finger as Zeke tumbled around and waved over to his friends on the other hand. The wind blew through Rai's fur as she closed her eyes. All the while, Zeke laughed, pointing and exclaiming.

Jeri rode in his right hand with Malachi and Fern, and she moved from side to side, making binoculars with her own hands, glaring out at the island.

They could see the ocean from the giant's hands, and its waves crashed against the island's shores. They could see multiple smaller islands sprinkled along the mainland coast. They passed through low, fluffy clouds, and the fog made everything disappear for a moment until it passed, allowing the bright sunlight to illuminate all of the tropical colors again. Flocks of colorful birds flew by, and one landed on the tip of Mesee's finger, the same finger that Rai clung to.

"Shoo!" she screamed at the bird, which sat unfazed, pecking its feathers and staring back at her.

She scooted herself up the giant's finger, holding tight with one arm and using her feet to push herself along. She waved her other arm toward the bird until it flew away.

They approached another mountain, one they had not seen the day before. It sat out in the distance ahead of them. As they rapidly moved closer to it, the mountain began to grow. While they passed by, the mountain awoke from its slumber and sat up, waving to the passing company with a gentle and kind smile. This mountain was a giant lady. Her hair fell like vines to the sides of her face, and the hand that waved was large and brown.

At this, Jeri glanced over at Malachi, and they shared a smile of both amazement and disbelief. Mesee had, in fact, been the mountain they saw and then lost the day before. He had awakened during their journey through the woods and moved without them knowing.

"Moving mountains, who would have thought?!" yelled Jeri to Malachi, shrugging.

Still holding tight to Mesee's hand, Rai opened one eye and then the other very slowly. She looked around at the beautiful landscape, and for only a moment, she cracked a small smile. Then Zeke jumped over to her, and she screamed and held tighter to the giant finger. Birds flew beside them as they dodged the bright white clouds that appeared, as though brushed by a giant's paintbrush among the clear blue sky.

"So, what does the place yous are looking for look like?" asked Mesee to Malachi, looking down at his hand where the boy sat.

"It's a large mill with a big house, a stream, and a water-wheel," he responded.

"Hmm," Mesee thought as he stomped through the forest.

"Me family, the Nausoris, have lived here in Fiji for many, many years," said Mesee, as he carried them. "We made our home here on the western coast, in Nadi, be-cause Mom loves the views of the ocean and the fancy resorts at Denarau Island...but me's never heard of Hobart Mill. It must be to the East. Is that one of those big, new hotels in Suva?"

"It's a very old flour mill in Tasmania. Maybe you've seen it before and forgot," said Malachi.

Mesee stopped in his tracks and looked down at the boy.

"Malachi, yous in Fiji. Tasmania is fars away," he said.

"Well, can't we go there?" said Rai, "You're, uh, big. You could get us there fast."

"Fiji is a island," said Mesee disappointedly. "It is sur-rounded by waters, deep ocean, no lands."

"Oh great!" shouted Rai as Zeke groaned and flung himself down on the giant's hand.

"Hold on, Mesee is thinking," said the giant as he stood still, holding the group suspended high above the ground.

As they sat in the giant's hands, floating above the tree-tops, Mesee stood still and looked as though he was in deep thought. They looked up and watched him as his giant eyelids began to flutter. Each time, it seemed his eyes would stay closed longer, and the suspense grew in the silence. He then let out a loud and roar-like yawn.

Mesee slowly shook his head from side to side, the way a stiff neck made of stone might move. As the vines of hair atop his head swayed back and forth, he slowly blew air between his closed lips, causing them to sputter and vibrate against each other. Sleepiness had overcome the giant, and it looked like he was trying everything to stay alert and upright.

"Is everything OK?" shouted Malachi up toward Mesee, cupping his hands around his mouth to project his tiny voice to the rather large ear of the giant.

"Oh yes, Mesee is great!" said the giant in response, smiling. "Thank yous for asking!"

It seemed as though the moment had not even fazed the giant. He continued as though nothing had happened, inattentive to the concern that soaked in the young boy's question.

"Mesee knows!" he finally shouted after a moment of thought. "Let us go!"

He carried them deeper into the jungle, where the trees seemed to get higher and more dense.

"Where are you taking us?" shouted a concerned and impatient Rai to Mesee.

"Sigatoka!" he responded, continuing to look forward. "But hey, while you is here, enjoy beautiful Fiji islands! Fiji is thought to be over 3,000 years old and beautiful!" said Mesee, in his tour guide voice. "This is our biggest island, Viti Levu, with cities here on the mainland like Nadi to the West and Suva to the East; beautiful resorts there. And for the more adventurous traveler, visit the barrier islands of Fiji, like Beqa, to watch the fire walkers! You will be amazed!"

"Fire walkers?" asked a stunned Jeri.

"Oh yes, fire walkers! Given the gift by the gods many, many years ago, this tribe can walk on red-hot coals and never burn their feet!" said Mesee.

"Let's go there!" shouted Jeri.

"This isn't a vacation, Jeri!" shouted Rai. She addressed the giant tour guide. "Thank you for the information, Mesee, but we must be returning to Hobart Mill."

"Not a problem, enjoy your stay. This is island time, friend!" Mesee responded.

Jeri pointed in the distance as they came closer to smoke funneling up into the sky.

"Yous will meet a lady in this village. Shes will be able to give yous food. She is Mesee's friend, and very wise and cans probably help yous with yous problems."

"Thanks for all your help!" said Malachi. "It would have taken us days to get here by foot!"

"No worries, little brother," said Mesee, as he blinked his eyes and let out a great yawn. "Mesee is happy to help friends! And please leave a good review for yous tour guide today. Again, Mesee Nausori is me name." The giant paused. "It won't be much longer!"

However, after a few more giant steps, Mesee began to waver from side to side as his eyes closed. Everyone held on to the large fingers of the giant, yelling to wake him up.

Mesee then opened his eyes wide and began to flutter his lips.

"Is everything OK?" shouted Malachi.

"All is great," responded Mesee, smiling. "Just a little sleepy."

He again fluttered his lips, seemingly to make distractions and keep himself awake.

"This explains the sleeping giant thing," shouted Rai.

The large eyelids of the giant began to close again, this time stopping him in his tracks as his body wobbled.

"Mesee!" shouted Malachi.

There was no response this time. The giant went deeper into his slumber, and his knees buckled, projecting his body forward toward the ground.

"Hold on tight!" yelled Malachi as they all screamed and tried to hold on to Mesee's giant fingers.

One by one, they fell from his hands as the giant crashed into the land, causing a huge shake on the surface of the solid ground. Mesee lay, with his arms stretched out, in a deep sleep. He had cleared all the trees that had once stood in his way and dozens of birds took off in flight, now swarming the skies above him.

Chapter Twelve

RAGING SIGATOKA RIVER

Malachi gasped for air as he opened his eyes. Pain shot through his back as the world around him slowly came back into focus. There was a loud, thunderous roaring sound, and he noticed the swift river that gushed directly below him. He held tightly to the large tree branch that now suspended him in the air at the river's edge. He sat up, wincing, holding tight to the branch. His arms were scratched up, and a cut on his forearm had begun to bleed. Looking around, he panicked, realizing he was all alone.

"Hello!" shouted Malachi.

"Hello!" he shouted again, trying to pull himself along the branch, back to the tree, and away from the swift river below him. "Is anyone here?" he shouted over the roar of the river's current.

His arms burned with pain. He heard something, a faint noise, but could not tell where it came from. He looked up in the tree and to his sides.

"Hey! Hey!" he heard someone grunt.

Malachi looked down a few branches to see Zeke and Rai waving, looking up at him as they clung to the branches of the tree.

"Hey! Hey!" Zeke grunted the words again.

They shouted at him, panic on their faces, but he could not hear them over the roaring noise.

"I can't hear you!" he shouted.

They began to point at the river and shout.

Malachi looked down at the water and could see Fern soaking wet. She was sitting, stranded, on a rock that sat in the middle of the raging river. Next to her, down in the water and trying to hold on to the rock as best as she could, was Jeri, drenching wet.

"Help!"

He could now, just barely, hear her faint cries.

Malachi looked around him and called to Zeke and Rai to join him on the branch.

"We have to save them!" he shouted to the Bogos as they worked to climb up the tree and closer to him.

"How?" asked Rai as she got closer.

"Um, follow me," he said.

Zeke and Rai slowly moved farther out on the large branch. They all watched the river below them rush by. Following Malachi's lead, they moved out farther and hovered over the water. They were closer to the rock where Jeri and Fern waited.

"OK, Zeke, I'll hold your feet and lower you down. You grab them, and I'll pull you back up."

"Ohh," grunted Zeke apprehensively.

"It'll be OK. I'll hold tight," responded Malachi.

Malachi grabbed onto one of Zeke's ankles and slowly lowered him down over the raging river and toward the rock where Jeri and Fern were stuck.

"Farther!" shouted Rai as she watched them.

Malachi stretched more and lowered Zeke as much as he could. He winced.

"I can't go anymore!" shouted Malachi. "We can't reach!"

He turned to Rai.

"Rai, you have to hang down too! Climb down to Zeke."

"I am not going down there!" she shouted.

"You have to! Hurry!" he shouted, his body stretching as he held to the branch with one hand and Zeke with the other.

The scratches and cuts on his arm hurt as he stretched.

Slowly, Rai began to climb down atop Zeke as Malachi continued to hold as tight as he could. She held Zeke's hand as she reached out toward Fern, who stood atop the rock.

However, as much as she stretched out her little furry arms, and as much as Zeke and Malachi stretched their whole bodies out, they still came too short. They wouldn't be able to reach the rock from the branch.

"Help, I'm slipping!" shouted Jeri, who still held to the rock as the water washed across her fur, unable to pull herself up onto the rock against the current.

Malachi used all his might to pull Zeke and Rai back up to the branch. He thought about what else could be done to save them. Suddenly, they all heard a scream as Jeri slipped from the rock and floated farther down the stream. The water pushed her into another rock that she quickly grabbed onto.

"Come on!" shouted Malachi as they raced to get out of the tree and made their way to the bank of the river.

As they approached the water's edge, Rai noticed a large mound on the opposite bank from where they stood. With shiny scales and a coiled body, the enormous snake was as thick as the trunk of the tree they had just hung from. It lay still on the shore of the river.

"Malachi, look!" shouted Rai, pointing across the river directly before them. "A giant snake!"

The serpent moved, awakened by the screams. As it began to uncoil its body and stretch out, it lifted its head. It had four serpent heads and the head of a human between them, and it opened all five sets of eyes to stare at them. It gazed out at the Bogo, who helplessly held on to the rock in the river. The snake's eyes glowed red as it slithered to the river's edge. As sly and smooth as anything Malachi had ever seen, it slipped into the water, its long body beneath the surface, and began swimming toward the rock and Jeri.

Jeri spotted the giant serpent making its way toward her. Malice shone clearly in the eyes of the serpent, which locked in on its prey. Its long, massive body swayed from side to side as it swam toward her.

Malachi, Zeke, and Rai watched from the shore, feeling hopeless as their friend fought to hang on while the serpent made its way at her.

The serpent was only feet from Jeri. Zeke closed his eyes, and they all screamed. From the opposite side of the river, a fin rose from the water's surface and made its way straight toward Jeri. Rai pointed and shouted.

"Shark!"

Jeri was cornered by the serpent and the shark, both racing in her direction.

The shark arrived first. Quickly, it began to circle the rock that Jeri clung to. As it swam, the water started to glow a bright blue. The glowing ring surrounded her, and the shark continued to circle.

The five-headed serpent approached, suddenly deterred. It couldn't cross the glowing blue circle, Malachi realized. It turned and swam away, leaving Jeri alone on the rock, still circled by the shark and the blue light.

The shark swam up to Jeri from behind, pushing her up on top of itself. She grabbed its fin as it swam her over to the rock where Fern lay, waiting for her rescue. Fern jumped from her rock into Jeri's arms, and the shark swam them closer to Malachi, Zeke, and Rai.

The shark, as it approached the shore, began to transform. It started to grow legs where there had been none, which it used to walk the two of them up onto the shore. It sat them down gently, and without a word, it turned and walked back into the water, where it again disappeared into the river.

"Thank you!" shouted Jeri, waving at the shark as its blue glow dissipated into the depths of the river.

"Are you OK?" asked Malachi to Jeri as he grabbed Fern and held her close.

"Whoa, that was frightening!" responded Jeri, as she wrung out her wet fur, "but really awesome! Let's do it again!"

"Absolutely not," responded Rai as she sat down and breathed deeply.

After a moment of rest, the group began heading toward the dark path Mesee had pointed out. He said it would take them somewhere safe, and more than anything, they wanted safety from the jungle that had already tried to take them down. They stayed close together while the bush around them grew more dense as they traveled the path. It was very dark, sunlight occasionally creeping in through the heavy canopy of branches covering them. The sunlight illuminated the leaves with bright green opacity. The sound of bugs buzzing set the soundtrack for their journey, and Malachi pulled out his flashlight from the backpack Jeri dragged behind her.

As usual, Zeke held the tail of the line as he occasionally stopped to pick up rocks along the path. He would closely inspect each one, bringing it close to his face, squinting to see it in the dark. He would smell the rocks, even lick them, and then decide if they were nice enough to put with his elite collection of other rocks from the path. He held tight to them all in his left hand.

"Hurry up, Zeke. Stay close to us!" shouted Rai, occasionally turning around and tapping her foot impatiently.

Zeke ran to catch up with them, dropping rocks as he fumbled about, groaning and sighing at Rai's constant complaints. Whenever she turned around, he would run back to pick up the rocks he had dropped.

A small stone near the path's edge caught Zeke's attention, and as he moved toward it, he looked up frequently to see if Rai had realized his absence. It was a smooth, round stone that shined with a blue sheen as the sunbeams made their way down through the trees' cracks. Zeke danced over to it. This rock looked much nicer than all the other rocks he had found. As he reached down to grab it, a rogue coconut smacked him in the head. He quickly looked up, shaking off the fruit's attack on him.

"Ow," he said, rubbing his head.

He reached down again, grabbed the rock, and held it close to his face. He stood there, admiring it, when another coconut came flying out from the edge of the forest, once again smacking into the little teal being.

"OW!" he shouted.

It knocked him down, and he jumped up, grunting and throwing one of the rocks back into the forest where the coconut originated. Not a second later, another coconut came straight at him.

He ran toward the rest of the group, unsure of what was after him. The coconuts continued to fly his way. He threw more rocks into the shadowed forest, a battle between him and the unknown attacker. Once he reached the group, the flying coconuts ceased. In his broken grunts and animated gestures, he tried to tell the group what had happened. Finally, panting, he pointed toward the trees, falling to the ground dramatically. Everyone stared at him as he gave up his pursuit and glared into the forest.

A moment later, as they all continued toward help, another coconut flew from the trees. This time, everyone saw it and it was followed by the bustle of branches and limbs. They all stopped and turned toward Zeke, who jumped up and down, pointing into the trees. They peered deeper and listened closer to the sounds of the forest. Their anticipation built as the sounds of breaking tree limbs and crunchy footsteps got closer and closer. The group huddled closer and closer together, now holding on to one another. The moment that the tension was at its highest point, out stepped the perpetrator.

She stood before them, ready for combat, with a coconut in each hand. Zeke immediately grunted at his rival, and the small girl threw a coconut right at him. He tumbled over in his predictable dramatic fashion. She stood as high as Malachi and looked about his age. She wore her hair long, and it shined like the midnight sky. Her eyes were large and green, and her cheeks were rosy from running. Her skin was darker than Malachi's, and she wore a blue and white uniform. Malachi jumped out quickly from the rest of the group and waved his hands as he approached the girl.

"Hey, stop that! We're not your enemy," said Malachi to the girl.

"What are those?" asked the girl, ready with a coconut pulled back behind her, using her other hand to point at the Bogos.

"They're my friends, and we would like it if you didn't throw things at us," said Malachi. "Can you drop the coconut, please?"

At that, the girl hesitantly placed the coconut on the ground, never taking her eyes off the creatures.

"I'm Malachi," he said, slowly approaching the girl for a handshake. "And they are the Bogos: Jeri, Rai, and Zeke. And that's Fern," he said, pointing to his trusty Tasmanian devil sidekick.

"Well, I've never seen anything like them," said the girl.

"They're really great. There is nothing to worry about with these guys, I promise," said Malachi, chuckling. The girl looked at the Bogos, then back at Malachi. Finally, her stern expression softened, and she smiled.

"I'm Shaniya," she responded. "Where are you from? I know I've never seen you in the village before."

"We're from Hobart Mill in Tasmania," said Malachi, "and we are here looking for someone to help us so that we can get back there. We were told there might be someone in the village who can help."

"Well, how did you get here?" she asked.

"We don't really know," said Malachi. "We kind of just arrived. One minute, we were at the shed at the mill, and then we were here."

"That is awfully strange," said Shaniya. "If I remember from my classes correctly, I think Tasmania is far from here."

"Yes, that's what the giant said before he dropped us at the river," responded Malachi, "and then Jeri was almost eaten by a snake before a sharkman saved her."

"Wait!" exclaimed Shaniya. "A snake? There aren't many snakes in Fiji that could eat you!" She laughed.

"It was a humongous snake!" shouted Rai. "Like, massive!"

"Really? Well, there is a large serpent named Degei, the greatest of all gods here in Fiji. But Degei wouldn't have tried to attack you like that. Perhaps it was Kaliya!" Shaniya gasped.

"It had five heads," said Malachi.

"Yes! That's him! You've been in the presence of the divine, Malachi. Kaliya is a Hindu naga, a deity, and not one to mess with. He was banished here to Fiji by Lord Krishna, and he lurks in the earth's bowels in Patala, the underground. Not many have seen him, ever. Much less above ground. His presence here on the island is only a legend to most."

"Well, he was in the river!" said Jeri.

"Big!" added Zeke.

"And then a sharkman, you said?" asked Shaniya.

"Yes," said Malachi. "And I know how it sounds. Crazy, right? But it was."

"Dakuwanga," responded Shaniya. "He is a Fijian god. A shapeshifter and protector. I'm glad he was there. You need someone like him to escape the wrath of Kaliya."

"No more snakes!" gasped Rai.

"Amazingly, you've seen them," she added. "But if Kaliya knows you're here, you should keep an eye out."

She thought for a moment.

"I think I know someone who can help you."

"Oh, great!" said Rai. "We could really use some help right now!"

"It's the Spoon Lady. She is the village shaman and the wisest person here. If anyone can help you, she can," said Shaniya.

"The Spoon Lady?" asked Jeri, in somewhat of a mock.

"She sounds like the weirdest lady if you ask me," said Rai. "Are you sure there's no one else?"

"Well, she is a little odd, so be prepared," said Shaniya, laughing. "But she'll be your best option for help. Come, I'll show you the way."

"Thank you, Shaniya," said Malachi as he turned and motioned for the rest of them to follow her.

Malachi picked up his backpack from the trail, where Jeri had dropped it during the attack, and then they followed Shaniya down the path. Zeke stayed in the back. He was still a little sour about his initial encounter with the girl, and he occasionally let out an exaggerated sigh or grunt while they walked. Fern took the lead beside

Shaniya, and she sniffed the air as they continued down the shadowed path. Malachi took Fern's trust in Shaniya as a good sign. Their hopes were high as they got closer to the village, where they would hopefully find the help they needed to return home.

Chapter Thirteen
A HOUSE OF SPOONS

Long before they reached the village that Shaniya had guided them toward, the smell of damp, fresh air mixed with the aromas of spices and smoked meat. The delicious aroma whiffed the noses of the group, becoming almost intoxicating. Unbeknownst to them all, they subconsciously had already quickened their pace. Their stomachs growled loudly, and their mouths watered as the hunger in them all took the lead.

Eventually, the path through the forest opened wide as they entered into the boundaries of a thriving village full of homes, animals, and families. The village was completely isolated from any other part of the island. Malachi thought it must be entirely self-sustaining, with its herders and butchers of livestock and growers and reapers of crops. Large black pots atop blazing piles of wood littered the yards of the homes as someone from each one cooked dinner.

They walked a jagged course between the modest tent homes, following Shaniya down a dirt path that cut through the center of the busiest intersections. Zeke dipped his finger into a few pots, hungry for a taste, as they all walked the path. He snuck up when no one was watching him, stopping to savor the hearty curry each time. However, Jeri turned around to catch Zeke in action, and she giggled. Jeri also ran up to one of the large black pots and glanced around quickly before sticking her finger into the thick sauce. They quietly laughed at their sneakiness together and ran to catch up with the rest, who were completely oblivious.

Near the center of the village, they passed by a simple cinder block one-classroom schoolhouse. The little white building's windows and doors were open wide as the tropical breeze blew throughout. The classroom was empty, as school had already finished for the day. Near the doorway stood a woman who appeared to be a teacher at the school. She was standing in the sliver of shade beneath the roof's overhang. All the schoolkids, still in their blue and white uniforms, were running around the front lawn, laughing and kicking up dust in a game of rugby.

They walked by many small homes, very simple and open. Toddlers ran through the dirt and grass, and older locals sat outside of their homes, huddled together while chatting and laughing loudly amongst one another. Many women were preparing big meals and carrying large pieces of meat and assortments of roots and other crops to the oversize boiling pots outside. The men of the village pushed around small herds of goats. A chicken sat atop the roof of one of the homes and gawked at them.

After they had walked through the middle of the entire village and were now at the opposite side, Shaniya stopped. They had left the central area, and from where they stood, only one home remained until they again entered back into the forest. This home was different from the rest of the homes they had seen. Objects were used to decorate the exterior, hanging from the doorway and off the roof.

As they approached the building, they saw that the items hanging from the sides were all shaped like spoons. Some were smaller, some more prominent, some made from stone, and some from wood, all different colors and styles. Nonetheless, they were all spoons. They completely covered the exterior of the home.

Standing by a large black pot, off to the side of the house, they spotted an older lady. She was mixing the contents of the pot as the fire beneath bellowed out clouds of gray smoke. Her bright, colorful dress was loose, ended right below her knees, inches above her bare feet, and was the color of vibrant indigo. Her lengthy black hair hung in a long single braid down the middle of her back, and weaved throughout it were strands of the same indigo from her dress. She wore a necklace with a small wooden teaspoon set amongst dozens of tiny purple beads. Her thin, wrinkled lips were stained plum, which brightly contrasted with her aged brown skin. The fringe on her forehead was messy and unkempt, almost covering her dark brown eyes. There was no denying that they had reached their destination.

"Bula!" shouted Shaniya with a smile as they approached the lady.

"Bula!" said the Spoon Lady in a husky, quivered voice, looking up from her pot and smiling. She raised her mixing spoon from the mixture and waved it at the group as bright, colorful ingredients ran from the spoon down to her hand.

"What does that mean?" whispered Malachi, grabbing Shaniya's shoulder and speaking under his breath so as not to be heard by the lady.

"'Bula' is a Fijian word. It's like saying 'hi,'" said Shaniya.

"B-Bulo. Erm...Bular!" shouted the group as they approached the Spoon Lady, somewhat hesitant and nervous, unsure if they were pronouncing the greeting correctly.

The older lady left her big black pot and, grabbing a tall, knobbed walking stick, she wobbled over slowly to meet them. She still carried the spoon in her hand as drips of purple lit up the green grass behind her. She smiled when she arrived before them, and her gleaming white teeth were illuminated against her dark plum-colored lips. The wrinkles around her lips and eyes exposed a kind history, one of laughter and wisdom.

"Hi, Shaniya," said the Spoon Lady as she approached them.

Shaniya waved and smiled as Malachi stepped up and reached out his hand to her, abruptly beginning to introduce himself.

"Ms. Spoon Lady, I'm Malachi Halladay."

She dropped her stick and reached out her hand, the one not holding the leaky spoon, and lightly held on to his. Her hand was fragile and tender, and she held on to him for a moment longer than he had expected. With the touch of her hand, she exuded a peace over him that helped to calm his anxiety, a peace that he had not felt in quite some time.

"My name is Marina," she said, smiling.

"Oh, I'm sorry. Nice to meet you, Marina," he responded.

"No worries," she laughed. "Everyone around here calls me the Spoon Lady, and hey, can you blame them?!"

And with that, she pointed at the spoon-covered house they all had noticed upon their arrival.

Malachi laughed nervously, unsure what to say, so he continued introducing the group.

"These are my friends, the Bogos," said Malachi, directing his attention to the small bundles of fur that stood behind him.

One by one, the Bogos stepped up to introduce themselves to the Spoon Lady named Marina. She bent slightly forward, reaching down to take their hands in hers, and smiled. Each time, she would follow up the introduction by saying, "It's a pleasure" or "Pleased to meet you."

When Marina spotted Rai, she gasped.

"Oh, I absolutely love the color of your fur!" Marina squealed, spinning Rai around in circles reluctantly as she gawked at the plum-colored fur covering the Bogo's body.

"We're twins!" Marina said with a laugh, pulling at her dress to compare.

Rai blushed.

Marina was extremely friendly to them, and her purple ensemble was bright in the midday sun. Her scent was sweet, and the spoon she held in her left hand continued to drip, causing a puddle of purple to stain the grass where she stood.

Once they had all become acquainted, Malachi turned to introduce Fern, who had disappeared from his side. She moved over to where Marina stood and licked at the puddle dripping onto the grass beside her.

"No girl, don't eat that!" shouted a concerned Malachi, reaching to grab her up.

"Oh, she's fine," said Marina. "It's only my mixture of longan fruit. It's quite tasty!"

"Here, try it!" she said, sticking the dripping purple spoon she held on to out in front of them.

"Oh, no thanks," he responded squeamishly.

Malachi backed away and let Fern continue.

"This is Fern," he said, pointing at the happy Tasmanian devil.

"Well, hello, Fern," she smiled, looking over at her.

"We have a problem," said Malachi abruptly to Marina, "and we are hoping you can help us somehow."

"Oh, is that so? And what happened to your arm?" she asked him, pointing down at the bloody cut on his forearm from the giant's fall.

"Just a little cut," he said, looking down at it and then trying to hide it from sight.

"Well, please, come inside," she said, walking toward the house. "I will make you some lunch, as you must be starving. Come rest. We can chat inside and get out of this hot sun. And I'll fix up that arm for you."

She warmly motioned for them all to follow.

They all walked behind her, including Shaniya, into the small, cozy home that belonged to the Spoon Lady. They sat down, making a circle with their bodies on the woven grass mat that covered the floor. There was not much in the room. They saw a small bookcase filled with big, old, dusty books. And on another shelf sat tons of little jars and bottles filled with various things. The contents differed in color and shape; some were filled with liquid, and some were not. The room was filled with many lit candles, illuminating the otherwise dark room.

Marina left them for a moment and came back with plenty of food. She passed around bowls of goat meat curry for them all to enjoy. They brought the bowls to their mouths, and each one fervently slurped down the meal, leaving their utensils to rest beside them. Shaniya helped Marina by handing out small cups of juice to each of them as they continued to devour their food.

Between slurps of curry, Malachi shared with Marina how they had all arrived in Fiji as she sat down beside him on a wooden stool and tended to his arm.

"We need to get back to Tasmania," he shared, "to Hobart Mill, where the Bogos live, and to Granny Annie's house, where I live."

"But that's a long way away, and we don't know how," Rai added with a mouthful.

"And how did you get here, to Fiji?" she questioned him as she took a large green leaf and wrapped it around his forearm.

"Well, we don't really know," added Jeri while wiping food from her fur. "There was this extremely bright light, and then we were sitting on a beach. Bottoms in the sand, and sand in our fur."

"Interesting," Marina responded. "Now, leaf this here for a while," she said as she tightly secured the leaf to Malachi's arm. Then she started giggling.

"Get it?! It's a joke!" she laughed, smacking her knee with her hand as she looked around at everyone else.

No one got it.

"It's a leaf, and I said, 'Leaf this here!'" she said, holding up Malachi's arm and shaking it for everyone to see.

"OK, never mind." She stopped giggling and looked at them.

"Why don't you all rest for a bit, and I'll think about it," she said as she got up and exited the room.

They all looked at one another and, in unison, started laughing.

Now that their bellies were full, each one of them began to yawn and spread out on the floor. The Spoon Lady may have been odd, but she was extremely kind and cared for them. Soon, the home was littered with sleeping adventurers, and Marina tiptoed across the floor, gently covering each one with tiny blankets, sure not to wake them. They were all exhausted from their day's trip and the lack of sleep they had each received in the jungle the night before.

About an hour later, after a fulfilling and much-needed nap, Malachi woke up to Fern licking his bottom lip. He smiled and pulled her close to him while stretching and yawning. He looked around the candlelit room and saw that all his friends were still sound asleep. He stood up and folded his blanket. Fern ran to the door, and he could hear talking outside. They exited the home through the back door to a covered sitting area where Marina and Shaniya sat. They were chatting away and giggling at each other's comments. He stood before them and rubbed his face, still trying to remove the sleepiness from his eyes.

"Good evening, Malachi," said Marina. "I'm glad you were able to rest."

"Yes, thank you very much," said Malachi.

"Have a seat and join us," she replied, as Fern jumped up in the seat beside Shaniya.

"Tell me more about your story. It sounds very interesting," said Marina. "I can imagine why you all were so tired. It sounds like you've come a long distance."

"Thankfully, we had some help along the way," he responded, sitting beside her. "There was this giant that found us in the forest. He helped us cover a lot more ground in a lot less time. He sent us to your village and said you could help us."

"A giant sent you my way?" she questioned. "Hmm, you must have met my dear friend, Mesee."

Malachi smiled at her and nodded.

"I just love chatting with him, but the poor guy suffers from severe narcolepsy," Marina said. "We can barely ever finish a conversation before he is passed out and shaking the island with his snoring!"

She laughed.

"Thankfully, he was awake long enough to tell us about you," said Malachi. "He carried us a long way but then fell asleep, and we were dropped from his hands near a river not far away from here. That's when I got this cut, actually."

"Oh yes!" Marina interjected. "Come here. Let me see!"

As he neared her, she unwrapped the leaf from his arm. As she pulled it away, he looked down to see that not only had the cut completely healed, but you could barely tell there ever was one.

"How did you do that?" he asked her, stunned.

"It's an old shaman trick." She smiled. "Do you feel re-leafed?"

They all looked at one another for a moment and began laughing.

"So what happened next on your adventure, Malachi?" asked Shaniya.

"Oh yeah, so then, Jeri and Fern landed in the river, the rest of us were in a tree, but then a huge serpent tried to eat her! Then there was a shark that came and saved them, a shark that grew legs!"

"Wow, what an experience!" Marina exclaimed. "It sounds like you've been in the presence of gods! I am so happy to see that you made it here safely. What a long day."

"Gods?" questioned Malachi.

"Oh yes, and you are lucky. It sounds like some of them are looking out for you and your friends. But I would watch out for that serpent, Kaliya. He isn't a nice one."

"Well, do you think you can help us return home?" Malachi asked.

"Malachi, I will try my best to get you and your friends back home," Marina said reassuringly as she reached over and patted his knee.

"For now, however, we must get ready for the par-TAY," she added as she started to dance in her seat.

"There's a party?" he asked.

"Yes, tonight! It is the night before Fiji Day, and we will celebrate at the schoolhouse. It will be a great time. Go and wake up your friends. We're gonna dance!"

"I don't know. We really should be getting back," responded Malachi. "I know Granny Annie will be worried until I get home, and I promised the Bogos I would get them home too."

"It's evening now, Malachi," said Marina. "It's too late to be out in the forest alone finding your way home. Especially if the gods know you're here. You'll be safe in the village, so enjoy the party and have fun. Come morning, I will help you all return to Tasmania. But for tonight, Malachi, just embrace this new adventure."

She smiled at him while she touched his shoulder, the moment resonating with a memory.

"I'm afraid to leave, Gwen. Can't I just stay with you?" asked Malachi.

Malachi sat on his bed in his room in New York City as his nanny, Gwen, helped him pack his final bag. It had been only days since his parents' funeral. Gwen folded each shirt from the chest of drawers and handed them to Malachi, who placed them in the luggage.

"Malachi, Granny Annie is looking forward to having you. She's your family and loves you so much," she said, stopping to sit beside him on the bed. Malachi sat beside her, quiet.

"You know, your parents couldn't wait until you were old enough to have your own adventures just like them," Gwen said. "And you want to know a secret?"

"What?" he asked.

"I think you're old enough now." She smiled. "You're such a brave person, and you've been so strong through all of this, Malachi. Your parents would be so proud of you, and so am I."

Malachi, although scared, wanted to make his parents proud more than anything in the world. With tears in his eyes, he forced a smile as they shuffled the luggage down the stairs and set them neatly by the front door.

"Can't you come with me?" asked Malachi, now looking up to Gwen. "I need you to come with me."

"You'll be OK, Malachi," she said. "I love you, and I am always here. Go and enjoy your adventure!"

Shaniya and Fern ran up to Malachi, Shaniya grabbing his hand to pull him along.

"Come on!"

Chapter Fourteen
SULUS AND KAVA ROOT

Shaniya, Malachi, and Fern entered the back door of the house.

"Wake up everyone! We must prepare for the party!" said Shaniya.

The little creatures began to stir and awaken from their dreams.

"A party? I think I love parties! I've never been to one, but it sounds super fun!" cheered a groggy and half-asleep Jeri, who pumped her arm in the air while still lying on the floor.

"What's a party for?" asked Rai, yawning.

"It's the night before Fiji Day!" said Malachi.

"And what's that?" responded Rai.

"It's uh, well, it's...," he said, unsure of his answer.

"It's the day we celebrate our independence as a country," added Shaniya. "We've been celebrating all week long to get ready for it. A lot of dancing, food, and fun stuff. You'll love it, and you are all invited!"

"Sounds like fun to me!" shouted Jeri, jumping up from her spot on the floor and grabbing Zeke's arm.

"Fun, fun!" shouted Zeke as he was pulled up from the floor.

"I thought Marina was going to help us get back home," said Rai to Malachi sternly.

"She will. She said she would," said Malachi.

"It doesn't seem like it. It seems like we're going to a party. How can we even trust this Spoon Lady?" questioned Rai. "Why doesn't she just tell us what she knows so we can go?"

"She has been nothing but nice to us, Rai," he responded. "Sometimes you just have to trust people. Not everyone is bad."

"But some people are bad, Malachi."

"You have to give her a chance," said Malachi. "She said it was late and that she would help us in the morning. It'll be too dark in the jungle alone now. The party will be fun."

"Fine," Rai huffed, "but I won't enjoy it."

"Come on, smile!" shouted Jeri as she danced around the room, twirling the blankets in her arms.

Marina entered the room and collected the tiny linens used as blankets. Using her handmade dye, created with the skins of the longan fruit she had boiled in the large black pot outside, she painted shapes and designs on them. She painted beautiful flowers, palm branches, and ocean waves. Then, one by one, she wrapped them around the waists of her guests, securing them with tiny pins.

"This is a beautiful dress!" exclaimed Jeri, as she spun around while the skirt-like clothing spun around her.

"Beauty!" shouted Zeke as he admired his own and began to twirl.

"It's a sulu!" laughed Shaniya. "Not a dress. Everyone wears them."

Zeke stood in the corner of the room wearing his sulu, spinning his around as he watched it drape around him. He spun until he lost his balance, falling over onto Rai.

"Oops," he muttered, regaining his foothold. Rai glared.

"A sulu is very important here in Fiji," added Marina as she pinned Rai's sulu. "It is one of our most traditional and formal attire. It shows respect to the local people when you wear it, and now you look like one of us!"

As Marina finished pinning, Rai looked down at her sulu and ever so slightly began to twirl it from side to side. She grinned. Malachi looked over at her, and as quickly as she could, she stopped smiling and huffed.

Once they had all finished preparing for the evening's festivities, they exited the small home together with Marina. The bright sun had lowered, and the heat was much more bearable. They returned through the village to the small schoolhouse they had passed earlier that day. Everyone in the village seemed to be out and about, dressed up and laughing in large groups. They all headed in the same direction that Marina was leading them.

The lanterns, lit with fire, burned along the village's main road. Beautiful and colorful flowers, deep reds and cotton candy pink, decorated the exterior of the homes, and tall bamboo shoots covered in beads and shells made up the bases of the lanterns. The sky was filled with hues of deep orange and golden yellow and was framed by the tops of the tall palm trees that swayed in the fresh evening breeze. The air blew through their fur and hair.

"Wow, everything is beautiful for Fiji Day," said Jeri as they walked the path to the schoolhouse.

"It's one of my favorite times of the year here in the village," said Shaniya. "We all get to celebrate what makes Fiji so beautiful: all of our different backgrounds and stories."

"What are your stories?" asked Rai.

Shaniya laughed.

"Well," she said, "my story is that I am Fijian but also Indian, or what you would call Indo-Fijian. My family is Hindu and celebrates many Indian traditions. But I am also Fijian. Our people came to this island long ago, and it has become our home."

"And I am a native Fijian," added Marina as she looked back and joined their conversation, carrying her tall wooden staff as she wobbled along the path. "So, my story is connected to my ancestors, who also grew up on this island. We celebrate a different kind of spirituality and have different customs than Shaniya and her family."

"Yeah, but on Fiji Day and the entire week around it, we come together and celebrate everyone who calls Fiji home," responded Shaniya.

"That's exactly right," added Marina.

"I love your stories!" exclaimed Jeri.

Lively, traditional music played ahead of them, and as they got closer to the schoolhouse, they heard people cheering. The atmosphere was happy, and everyone wore smiles and rejoiced. When they saw the group of newcomers, most people shouted "Bula" and waved to Malachi, Marina, Shaniya, Fern, and the Bogos. However, many people stopped to stare at them. A group of women even shrieked in surprise at their unusual appearances.

"Oh, they're fine!" said Marina, laughing, to the locals who showed concern at the sight of them. "Friends of mine. Nothing to worry about. Nothing to see here. Move along, move along. Shoo."

She motioned with her staff, swinging it from side to side.

Men and women stood outside, under a covering beside the school, with various instruments, including drums, ukuleles, and guitars. They played beautiful rhythms as others danced around them and sang. Shaniya grabbed

Malachi's hand and pulled him over to the space where the others danced. The two of them laughed as they jumped around and danced to the energizing music of the native Fijian band.

Marina stopped to speak with a friend while the Bogos walked ahead to the long line that jetted out of the schoolhouse. As the line moved and the Bogos inched up to the doorway, they could see the pots and pans lining the tables inside. The people of the village filled their plates with food, and the smell inside was wonderful.

"Yum!" growled Zeke as his stomach rumbled. "Eat!"

The three of them grabbed their plates, and unable to see into the pots atop the tables due to their heights, they reached upward, putting the spoons down into the pots and pulling out lumps of food, a mystery until it hit their plates. They piled their plates high and full. Zeke stopped at a pot too high for him to reach, but a kind older man scooped some cassava onto Zeke's plate for him and smiled.

"Thanks!" said Zeke, with his one-toothed smile back.

After exiting the building, they found a narrow spot on a bench at a table outside. They scrunched in amongst the others, and, not wasting a second, they quickly devoured the heaps of food that covered their plates. The Fijians at the table with them watched with wide eyes, amazed and intrigued by the fuzzy creatures and their eating habits.

With their food gone and bellies full, the villagers at the table began to pass around a large wooden bowl filled with what they called "kava." They passed it from person to person, bringing the bowl to their mouths and drinking from it, then passing it to their neighbor on the left.

"Bula!" the men shouted at every sip.

When the bowl got to the three little creatures, they stared down at the murky brown liquid inside. Jeri sipped first, then Zeke and Rai followed hesitantly.

"Ugh," they said, sticking out their tongues and attempting to wipe the taste away.

At first, nothing seemed to come of it except that it filled their mouths with a taste resembling the smell of feet. However, as the bowl continued to be passed around and everyone took more sips, including the Bogos, their tongues slowly began to numb. Jeri stuck hers out and touched it with the tip of her finger.

"I can't feel my tongue," she said, with a lisp.

"Me either," lisped Rai.

Zeke blew raspberries in the air.

They looked at one another and laughed, and they continued to sip from the bowl until Marina noticed them from across the lawn. She hastily hobbled her way over to them with her staff, tapping them on the shoulder.

"OK, I believe that's enough kava for you all."

She helped the Bogos up from their seats and assisted Zeke with his sulu, which had come undone and now dragged at his ankles. She watched them as they stumbled away in their makeshift garments. Looking back at the men at the table, she pointed at them and smiled, shaking her head.

The men laughed.

Meanwhile, Shaniya and Malachi had found a group of kids to play with. Malachi recognized them as the kids who had been playing rugby earlier that day when they had first passed through the village. They all sat together in a circle on the ground as one of the boys made them all laugh at his jokes.

"What did the vampire lizard say?" he asked.

They all stared at him.

"Iguana suck your blood!" he answered in his best vampire voice, jumping up to launch toward them.

Some kids screamed and laughed, while others booed at their friend's cheesy joke.

The music that had been playing in the background ceased as the village band left the stage to take a break. As they did, the Bogos stumbled over to the stage, picking up the instruments left behind. They started to play the familiar tune that Malachi had first hoard resonating from the shed at the mill. This time, however, it was faster. It was obvious they were playing for a party. Everyone cheered as the Bogos played and sang, beating on the drums and harmonizing. People began to get up and dance again, and the group of kids pointed at them from where they sat.

"Hey, aren't those your friends?" asked one of the girls.

Malachi and Shaniya started laughing and nodded their heads.

"They're very good!" said another one of the kids in the group. "I really like this!"

"I didn't even know they could play real instruments!" said Malachi.

The rest of the village band came back up and joined them, and as the sun slowly disappeared behind the palms and dusk fell, everyone danced to the sound of the music and the light of the burning lanterns.

As the evening passed, a slow drizzle of rain began to fall, and it became heavier by the minute. Everyone cleaned up the instruments and food and retired to their homes for the night. The air was fresh and damp, and the rain had cooled down the extreme heat from the bright Fijian sunny day.

The band shook the Bogos' hands as they left after they had helped to take the instruments inside and out of the rain. Rai and Jeri, who hadn't yet noticed Zeke's absence, heard loud voices coming from the field near the school. Malachi, Shaniya, and the other village kids had begun another game of rugby. Rai and Jeri heard laughing and yelling while their game continued despite the wet field and rain.

A loud cheer exploded from the field, and as Rai and Jeri looked over to see what new excitement had transpired, they spotted the soaked teal fur of the Bogo they had all come to love. Zeke was out in the midst of the crowd. Holding the ball in his arms, he ran around, dodging the kids' launches and racing down the field. Jeri laughed huge belly laughs and took off running towards the field. She grabbed a reluctant Rai's hand and pulled her along.

Shaniya, Malachi, and Fern ran after the others as Rai and Jeri joined in. They played in the field with the kids until the setting sun gave off no more light. They chased one another and enjoyed one another's company. Malachi got to know his new friend Shaniya, who now loved the Bogos and carried Jeri on her shoulders down the field.

"Go, go!" they all shouted as Shaniya and Jeri made their way toward the goal line with the ball.

"Score!" Jeri cheered as she jumped to the ground and smacked the ball against it.

"Way to go!" shouted Shaniya, giving Jeri an energetic high five.

Zeke yelled excitedly, throwing himself on the wet grass and rolling around.

They all huddled together to congratulate the winning team and smiled as they enjoyed the company of new friends. One by one, they told all of the village kids good-bye and headed back toward the spoon-covered house, dirty and wet. Marina stood outside as they walked up to her, handing out towels. She dried the Bogos and helped pick the grass from their fur.

They all sat around under the covering outside, wrapped in their towels and blankets, as the rain fell. Marina, the Spoon Lady, told stories that made them laugh and hold on to their seats. They spent the rest of the evening giggling and enjoying their time, just being calm and carefree, completely forgetting, if only for a moment, that they were still thousands of miles away from home.

Chapter Fifteen

AN OLD HAT BOX

As the sun rose high and bright the next morning, the gawking chicken from the day before belted out his morning greeting from the rooftop. Malachi stirred at the sound, and as he did, he could feel Fern doing the same beside him. He reached over, rubbed her head as she opened her beady eyes, and let out a big yawn, showing all her pointy teeth.

"It sounds like Beep from home, doesn't it?" he said, petting her. He sat up at the sound of Marina entering the front door.

They had, all again, fallen asleep scattered across the main room floor. As Malachi looked around at everyone else stirring in their sleep, the little mounds of blankets, he saw Marina smiling at him as she closed the door behind her.

"Good morning!" she said, holding a huge basket. "I went out to get some fresh fruit for breakfast, and it smells delicious!" She lifted the basket to her face and sniffed.

The door opened again behind her, and Shaniya entered the home.

"Good morning!" she said to Malachi, who still sat in the middle of the room. "Marina, can I help you with breakfast?"

"I'll help, too," said Malachi, getting up from the floor and stretching.

"Absolutely!" responded Marina. "There is plenty to do! It will be a breakfast feast!"

Once in the kitchen, they peeled and cut up the fresh melon, pineapple, mangoes, and guavas. The colors of the fruit were bright like the morning, and the fresh juice that dripped from each one had the kitchen smelling vibrant. As Malachi and Shaniya helped Marina in the kitchen, they sipped from the milky coconut Shaniya had brought over, sent with her by her mother.

Soon, the kitchen was filled with sleepy and straggling Bogos, one by one, as they woke up and picked at the array of fruits laid out for them, buffet style, on the kitchen counter.

Marina suddenly made a surprised noise.

"Oh!" She wiped off her juice-covered hands with a kitchen cloth. "Before I forget, I have something for you, Malachi!" she said, cheerfully waving her arms up in the air. "It completely slipped my mind! Why don't you all go sit outside with your breakfast, and I'll bring it out?"

With that, she disappeared into a room down the hallway. Malachi, Shaniya, and the Bogos put fruit on their plates and went outside to the covered room where they had sat the night before. They looked at one another, wide-eyed, curious about what she may bring back. They continued to share the sweet juice of the coconut, which they drank straight from the fruit's shell.

A few moments later, Marina reappeared at the doorway of the home, holding a dusty, round brown box in her hands. It was a hat box, Malachi realized. He looked up at Marina with a large, confused grin and glanced back over at Shaniya, who gave a quick shrug of her shoulders.

"What is it? What's the surprise?" asked Jeri, bouncing on her seat with a mango in hand, gawking over at the box.

"Surprise!" grunted an excited Zeke beside her.

Looking down at the brown box that sat in his lap, Malachi slowly removed the lid to reveal the hat that lay inside. It was a bit dirty and the color of khaki, with a full brim that wrapped all the way around. It looked like it was made for an African safari or exotic jungle expedition. This hat was usually used on an adventure alongside binoculars and a pair of tall, laced boots. The hat was very worn, demonstrating the wear of many journeys it had traveled. But it had been in storage for some time and smelled of old, stale dust.

"Thank you," he said, forcing a smile to hide his confusion at why he had been chosen for such a unique gift.

"You are very welcome," responded Marina, the Spoon Lady, with noticeable excitement.

Malachi continued to front a nervous smile and slowly put the lid back on the box. Why had she given him this hat? What was its significance?

"It belonged to your father, Kristofer," Marina said.

And with that statement, Malachi's entire attitude changed. He looked back down at the box, again removing the lid and seeing the dusty hat.

He grabbed it.

He stared at it for a moment.

He pulled the hat close to him as he looked back up at her.

"How? You knew my father?" he asked her, desperate for an answer.

"I did," Marina responded. "I considered your father, Kristofer, a dear friend. He visited here with me many years ago. He accidentally left this hat behind, and I've held on to it ever since. I kept it safe from the moths and weather. I hoped I would get the chance, one day, to return it to him."

"Now you can return it to him, Malachi!" said Jeri. "This is great!"

"I can't," he said, holding the hat. "I can't give it to him."

"Well, why not?" inquired Rai. "It doesn't seem too difficult."

"Because," responded Malachi, as he stared down at the hat in his hands. "Because he died. Because they both died. My mom and dad are gone."

It was the first time he had ever had to say those words out loud.

"Oh," sighed Jeri.

"I'm so sorry, Malachi," added Rai.

A moment of silence passed as Malachi faced his emotions.

"I'm sorry to hear about your parents, Malachi," Marina said softly.

"My father was here? I don't even know what to say," said Malachi, still holding tight to the hat. "This is so unbelievable. Thank you, Marina."

"You are very welcome," she said. "You know, when Kristofer showed up at my door many years ago, it was a lot like you did yesterday. Curious, seeking answers from me."

"Why was he here? Was he alone?" questioned Malachi.

"No, actually, he had a creature very similar to you all." Marina pointed at the Bogos.

"A Bogo?" asked Malachi.

"Yes, exactly," she responded. "He was on a journey similar to the one you are on now." Malachi and the Bogos stared at Marina.

"Malachi, it is not an accident that you are here on this island, befriending these creatures, visiting with me," Marina continued. "You are here because you have been chosen, just like your father, Kristofer, was."

"Chosen? Chosen for what? By whom?" he asked, almost breathless.

"Jeri," said Marina, turning her attention to the creature. "Can I see that little yellow book of yours?"

Jeri's eyes widened, and Rai's mouth gaped open.

"Um." Jeri was hesitant.

"Don't," demanded Rai to Jeri.

"Trust me, I can help you," she assured them.

Jeri slowly pulled out the little yellow book from her fur almost magically, as if she had pockets built into the dense, colorful fuzz that covered her entire being. It was the same book she had shown Malachi in the jungle two nights before. Jeri slowly handed the book over to Marina.

"This guidebook will contain all of the answers you need," Marina said, holding it up in front of the group.

"I already read it the other night," responded Malachi.

Rai's eyes bulged at that, and she stared at Jeri disappointingly.

"There is not much in it," Malachi continued. "Just many empty pages."

"Shh!" Jeri hushed him and put her finger to her lips.

"Really?" Marina responded as she flipped through the pages until she found what she was looking for.

"Here it is," she said, handing over the small yellow book to Malachi.

Malachi was amazed as he looked down at a page full of text. This page had not existed the night when Jeri had shown it to him.

"THE WANDERING DOOR," he read the title on the page to himself.

"Read it for us," Marina added.

Malachi began to read the new text out loud to the group.

THE WANDERING DOOR IS A GIFT FROM THE KEEPER OF LIGHT. IT EXISTS TO LEAD BOGOS ON THEIR QUESTS, AND THEY CAN SUMMON IT WHEN NEEDED. IN ORDER TO ACCESS IT, THEY FIRST HAVE TO FIND THE DOOR ITSELF, WHICH IS NOT ALWAYS EASY. THE WANDERING DOOR CAN ONLY BE ACCESSED WHEN BOGOS AND THEIR TRAVELERS WORK TOGETHER.

ONCE THE WANDERING DOOR HAS BEEN OPENED IN A NEW PLACE, ITS SHADOW WILL EXIST IN THAT

PLACE FOREVER. PAST SHADOWS OF THE WANDERING DOOR EXIST ALL OVER THE WORLD, AND BOGOS AND TRAVELERS CAN TRAVEL BETWEEN THEM OVER AND OVER AGAIN.

HOWEVER, ONLY ONCE IN THEIR LIFE CAN A BOGO OPEN A BRAND-NEW DOOR AND CREATE A NEW SHADOW: A NEW PATH FOR ALL BOGOS AND TRAVELERS TO ACCESS IN THE FUTURE. OPENING THE WANDERING DOOR REQUIRES A BOGO, A TRAVELER, AND A TRAVELER'S KEY. WITHOUT THEM, THE KEEPER OF LIGHT IS THE ONLY BEING WHO CAN OPEN A NEW DOOR.

TRAVELING THROUGH THE WANDERING DOOR MEANS ARRIVING AT THE INTERSECTION OF PHYSICAL AND IMAGINED REALITY. WITHIN THIS REALM, THE WORLD IS SEEN NOT ONLY WITH THE EYE BUT WITH THE CREATIVE MIND. THE WORLDS BEHIND THE DOOR ARE WORLDS WHERE INDIVIDUAL AND CULTURAL IMAGINATION, FOLKLORE, AND TALL TALES COINCIDE WITH NATURE. THE KEEPER OF LIGHT KNOWS THAT IMAGINATION, FAIRY TALES, AND MYTHOLOGY ARE JUST AS REAL AS THE WORLD YOU CAN SEE DAILY. THE WANDERING DOOR AND ITS SHADOWS ARE GIFTS TO EXPLORE ALL TRUTHS.

FOR, IS THE TRUTH OF ONE'S MIND NOT THE TRUTH OF ONE'S REALITY?

THROUGH ALL WANDERING, THE KEEPER OF LIGHT WILL ALWAYS BE YOUR GUIDE.

"Whoa!" expressed Jeri excitedly.

"And this, Malachi, is why no airplane will get you home," said Marina. "The magic you experience here is unlike what you experience back in your world. Because, as much as this may look like the world you know, it, in fact, is not. This is a place you've always known about but have never been able to see or experience yourself. Here, things like dreams, legends, and lore show themselves externally, not just within the minds of those who think or believe it."

"How am I here? How does this even exist?" questioned Malachi. "And how am I supposed to get home?"

"Malachi, you possess the same adventurous spirit that your father had," she said, smiling at him. "He had many of the same questions when he and I met. Unfortunately, this is your adventure, not mine. And even if I could give you all the answers you seek, I wouldn't. That wouldn't be fair to you. You must determine your own fate and create your own journey in life. That is not for me to do. But, I will help guide you as much as I can."

"Yes, please, just help me get home," responded Malachi.

"I had a dream last night, and I know how to get you home," said Marina as she closed her eyes in a Zen state.

"A dream? That's the answer?" questioned Rai.

"Just listen," hushed Jeri. "Look, she's in her zone!"

"To get you back home to Tasmania, you must find a shadow of the Wandering Door, much like the one you arrived here through. And you must find it together. You will need to journey through the jungle, leading you all onward to a southern point of the main island: the Coral Coast," said Marina to the group.

"But we didn't get here through a Wandering Door," responded Rai. "We don't even know what that looks like. It just happened!"

"Yeah, exactly," added Malachi.

"You didn't? Are you sure about that?" questioned Marina, opening one eye to peer at them.

"Well, if it was the Wandering Door, we definitely didn't know about it," Malachi added.

"Hmm. Then you've been summoned, my friends," she said, closing her eyes again.

"Summoned? By who?" questioned Malachi.

"The Keeper of Light, of course," she added.

Marina smiled as she continued her story.

"Once you've all reached the Coral Coast, you will look for a shoal leading you to a rocky islet off the shore. I believe it is on that islet that you will find your way back home."

She sat there, swaying side to side with her eyes closed.

Marina's story would have seemed a bit unlikely to Malachi a few days ago. But, given the situation he currently found himself in, it seemed like the most believable solution he had. He and the Bogos had no other ideas at this point. If he wanted to find his way home and get them back home, he would have to choose to trust Marina.

Suddenly, she opened her eyes and looked at them.

"I cannot guarantee that this will all work out for you, as there will be decisions made along the way that are not up to me," she added, looking at Malachi. "You will have to be your own guide, with the help of these creatures alongside you."

She could tell there was doubt and concern among the faces of the group.

"Sometimes, the magic of life is stronger and much closer than you ever thought," said Marina, smiling back at them. "Just give yourself the grace to explore new things and, while you do, rely on the help of those who journey with you."

They all gazed at Marina until Malachi spoke up.

"How did you know about the book?" he questioned her suspiciously.

"As I said, these are not the first Bogos I have met," she responded.

"And the book said that the Wandering Door can only be opened by Travelers. How will we access it without one?" he further questioned her.

"Who said you're without one?" she questioned him while she handed over the packed food she had prepared for them to take on their journey.

Malachi shoved the wrapped packages into his back-pack.

"The forest out of here has become a bit overgrown, as no one ever takes the back way out anymore. So the path will be difficult to follow," she said.

"I can show them the way out," said Shaniya, smiling over at the others. "I've explored the forest many times. I can join them until they reach the clearing on the other side. My mother won't allow me to go any farther than that."

"If you don't mind doing that, Shaniya, that would greatly help our new friends," said Marina.

"Thanks, Shaniya!" added Malachi, followed by the gratitude of the others.

"Thank you so much for everything, Marina. You've been very helpful!" said Malachi.

"You are all very welcome," she responded. "It has been a true joy and pleasure to meet you."

Marina gave them each a big bear hug, sending them on their way. When she got to Malachi, she looked at him and reassured him with a smile and a nod. She held the sides of his face in her hands and looked into his eyes. She bent down and then embraced him.

"Your parents would be so proud of you," she whispered in his ear. "You are a very brave leader. Enjoy your adventure."

Malachi embraced her with a tight hug and then grabbed his father's hat, placing it on his head. He was still in awe that his father had once been to the same village he was visiting. Even more shocking was that his father had known Marina and that she had held on to his hat for so many years.

"Now listen, Malachi," she said, looking at him directly. "You must hurry and be on your way. You can, and will need to, reach the Coral Coast by sunset and find the shoal. The sandbank that will be your bridge to the islet only exists when the tide is low. As the tide rises with the setting sun, you will lose access to the islet by the ocean waters and will be forced to stay another night and day here in Fiji. And I cannot guarantee your safety, nor would I want you to wait for the dangers lurking in the jungle by night. You all made it through one night in the jungle," she added. "Let's not test out your luck."

She smiled and patted his shoulder.

Fern jumped up and ran ahead of him, stopping to look back before she began circling Jeri's feet, who had also already run ahead. Marina handed Rai another sack of goodies for the trip she had collected from the party the night before.

"And for you, Zeke," said Marina, turning to him. "I made this for you."

Marina showed him a handmade necklace, complete with dyed purple string. A substantial wooden spoon hung on the necklace, with little wooden beads surrounding it.

"I noticed you looking at mine," she said, pointing to her spoon necklace that hung around her neck, "so I decided to give you one of your own."

She placed the necklace over his head so that it hung around his neck. He was awed by it, becoming oblivious to everything else, wobbling in circles and struggling to keep his balance. He looked down, staring at the spoon that hung around his neck.

"Thanks!" he grunted with his big, humbled one-toothed smile.

He ran to catch up with the others.

Shaniya walked with them to the edge of the trees, holding back a large tree branch until the clear and open village converged into a dark pathway into the forest. Marina stood and watched as she bid farewell to the group, smiling and waving as they disappeared into the bush one by one. Zeke stopped one last time to dip the spoon that hung on his necklace into a delicious pot of food outside of one of the homes. He waved his spoon in the air as he ran to catch up with the rest.

Malachi turned around to wait for Zeke, and as he did, he looked up, gave one last smile, and waved to Marina in the distance. Zeke ran past him, and Malachi turned back around, slowly disappearing from her sight. He followed behind his friends down the path in the woods as Shaniya took the lead. He trusted Marina, hoping their path would lead them to the door, which he hoped would return them home.

Chapter Sixteen

THE SWAMP IS ALIVE

The day was still early, and according to Marina, they had a while to travel before arriving at the Coral Coast. Birds chirped songs in the trees, and the warm sunlight infiltrated through the cracks of the forest's ceiling above them. It had now been two nights that they had spent away from their homes. Malachi had enjoyed his last few days, the things he had seen and the people he had met. However, when he thought of Granny Annie back home, he worried. He could only imagine what she was thinking and feeling and how concerned about him she must be.

As he mindlessly followed along the overgrown path, with deep thoughts fogging his mind, he wondered if Marina's plan would work for them.

What if I get stuck on this distant island forever?

He could feel himself getting overwhelmed and anxious. Marina's home had been comfortable for him, and she had felt so familiar, but now that they were back on their own again, it was up to him to lead himself and the Bogos to home, and safety. Homesickness rose inside of him, and he felt uneasiness in his stomach. He closed his eyes for a moment of peace and took a few deep breaths, trying his hardest to conceal his nervousness from the rest of the group. Then he marched forward.

As they continued through the forest, they stopped regularly for breaks and snacks, as the Bogos' little legs had to double-step to keep up with Shaniya's. He watched the Bogos as they followed, remembering they, too, were far away from their homes. Zeke took turns getting piggyback rides from the group, and by that, meaning mostly Malachi. Rai carried Malachi's backpack and took pleasure in rationing the snacks out. Malachi knew that she liked being in control of stuff. She was responsible, and although it seemed like she lacked fun at times, she was good at it. She was a protector, for sure. She cared a lot about the others, just like Malachi. She even smiled at him from time to time now but would quickly stop as soon as she realized what she was doing.

Being the magical, musical creatures they are, the Bogos never let a dull moment pass by. For their entire trip through the jungle, they sang, given any opportunity, the music that seemed to play within their souls constantly. The trio used anything they found as a musical instrument: coconuts, small stones, and even sticks dragged against the bark of the trees. Malachi was grateful. It helped keep their spirits high and fear low and even soothed Malachi's mind. It also helped to pass the time and keep everyone awake and alert. Their organic melodies held every essence of a magical excitement: calming yet energizing.

The hard, beaten path that had led them from the village grew more obscure. It was apparent that it had been quite some time since anyone had traveled this far into the wild jungle. The plants were overgrown and crowded the short travelers along the way. Malachi and the group ripped through large and sturdy vines and pushed down small shrubs as they managed their way through. The jungle was more dense than ever.

Finally, they noticed that the ground beneath their feet had begun to soften, no longer like the packed dirt path they had walked earlier that day. With each step, the ground beneath them gave way, and their feet sank deeper into the damp earth. To keep from sinking farther into the sludge, they stepped on big dead vines that dropped down from massive trees and onto rotten logs. Malachi encouraged them to grab onto low-hanging twigs and branches to keep their balance.

"Be careful; it's very slippery here!" shouted Shaniya back to the group as she tried to keep her balance crossing over a giant log.

Malachi noticed that Fern had disappeared from his side, and as he looked back, he could see her standing behind him on a sturdy, elevated root from one of the ancient trees. She pawed at the ground around her and looked from side to side, unsure where to step. She whimpered. Malachi took a few steps back and scooped her up in his arms.

"Come here, girl, it's OK," he whispered as he picked her up.

He tucked Fern under his left arm and held her tightly as he used his right arm to hold on to the vines and tree trunks. He and Shaniya held branches aside as the Bogos made their way through the forest.

The overgrown swampy mess was becoming too thick to trek through. As their footprints sunk more and more, they tried their hardest to push through. It quickly became apparent that they could not go much farther. Shaniya turned around to look at them all, thinking of a different route, when she noticed the jungle around them had begun to thin out just a bit. She could see that, just past the heavy, overgrown pathway, there was a clearer path ahead.

"It looks like we may be almost done with the worst of it!" she said as she pointed out in front of them. "It looks much clearer just ahead."

With a few more steps and a lot of fighting against nature's wall of leafy green clusters, they stepped out into a much less dense area of the swamp. But just because they had escaped the trees didn't mean they had escaped the mud. A strong, strange, unwelcome fragrance filled the air as they looked out at an enormous puddle of muddy brown swamp that surrounded them.

"Zeke!" exclaimed Rai, covering her nose, implying the smell was coming from him.

"Wha?" groaned a confused Zeke as Jeri and Malachi chuckled.

"I don't think it's Zeke," said Malachi, holding his nose. "It looks like we have come up upon a swampy area. I think it's the smell of old mud."

The swamp ahead of them was bare and boggy. The plants that grew there differed from what had been on the path earlier. The soil was watery and darker in color. With another step, Rai lifted her foot in disgust, now coated in inches of wet mud. They could not go much farther unless they wanted to swim.

"Now, where should we go?" asked Malachi. "The path led us straight to a dead end. There's no way we can cross this."

The group looked around for alternative options, but the swamp was large, and there was no path. The forest was overgrown and thick, and there was no other space to travel outside the path where they stood.

"Fun!" shouted Zeke.

Everyone turned around to find Zeke lying on his back in the mud, flapping his arms and legs, making mud angels. Jeri laughed, shrugging, and flopped down to the ground, joining Zeke. They laughed and played as the thick mud caked their fur.

Rai tiptoed around at the edge where the path met up with the swamp, trying out the ground before her in search of a stable path to cross. She felt around, stretching her leg out and tapping the ground beneath with her toes.

"There's nowhere to go," she exclaimed. "We've come all this way for nothing."

Zeke pulled himself out of the suctioning mud and looked down at his impression on the ground.

"Me!" he yelled, smiling at the ground as his fur dripped with mud.

He then took off, running out toward the large swamp.

"Don't go too far!" shouted Shaniya. However, within a few feet, Zeke suddenly sank so far into the mud that only his arms and head were above the surface. The entire bottom of his body was submerged.

"Help! Help me!" the little teal creature managed to get out in his slurred speech.

"Zeke!" screamed Rai, watching as he slipped down into the earth.

She ran after him but suddenly sank down to her waist. She was only a few feet away from where Malachi was standing, and he reached out and grabbed her, pulling her back out from the mud before it took hold.

"Careful, you'll sink too!" he gasped.

"What are we going to do?" Rai shouted as she paced back and forth, throwing her hands up in the air.

"Help," groaned Zeke. He had sunk even more.

"We have to hurry. Let's get him!" shouted Jeri anxiously. She was still covered in mud from making mud angels with Zeke.

"Is there anything around that we can use?" asked Shaniya. "Look around."

Malachi looked around for a moment. The Bogos were looking to him to save their friend, but the mud would surely suck him in, too, if he were to walk out to Zeke. He placed Fern down on a stump and walked to the swamp's edge, where his feet began to sink to his ankles. He stepped back and grabbed a long stick off of the ground.

"Here, grab this!" he shouted as he held the stick out as far as he could from the edge of the swamp.

Zeke tried grabbing at the stick. Malachi pushed it farther out as his feet began to sink in again, stretching his arm out to its fullest extent.

"Grab on!" shouted Malachi to Zeke as he stretched his body to uncomfortable limits and gritted his teeth.

Zeke, flailing his arms around, finally could reach and grab onto it.

"Yay! Good job!" shouted Jeri as she began clapping.

Rai watched through the gaps in her fingers as she covered her face in suspense.

Malachi pulled on the stick, and slowly, Zeke began to rise out of the mud. Malachi pulled with all his efforts, and his whole body leaned backward as he pulled the little creature slowly out of the boggy swamp.

Shaniya ran over to help, but before she could reach Malachi...

Snap!

The old, rotten stick snapped in half, sending the boy backward onto the ground behind him as Zeke sank back down into the mud, this time sinking down farther.

"Zeke!" shouted Rai.

"What do we do now?" shouted Jeri, jumping up and down. "Do something, Malachi!"

The Bogos had put all their hope in the boy, and the pressure was heavy. Malachi began to panic as Zeke yelled out from the mud.

Then, Shaniya remembered the tangly vines they had fought as they made their way through the jungle.

"The vines!" she shouted.

She ran back to the edge of the trees and found a sturdy green vine. She picked it up and tied it securely around Malachi's waist. He walked to the edge of the swamp and, step by step, began to sink in the mud as he walked toward Zeke. The other Bogos and Fern watched as Malachi sank little by little as he trekked farther into the thick mud that had swallowed their friend.

Once Malachi reached Zeke, only the creature's eyes and teal and black fur on the top of his head could be seen. Malachi reached down in the mud, grabbed hold of Zeke, and pulled him up as forcefully as his body could. Shaniya pulled on the vine and began pulling the two out of the mud. However, as she pulled, it seemed the mud fought back and pulled them down farther. Suddenly, the vine snapped as Zeke sank out of sight, and Malachi went with him.

An eerie silence covered the swamp. They all watched, speechless, and the earth bubbled in digestion.

"No!" shouted Rai. She ran up to the swamp's edge as Jeri watched in disbelief from the stump, where she sat holding Fern. Shaniya stood holding the broken vine in her hand.

"What do we do? What do we do?" shouted Rai as she paced back and forth, looking at both Shaniya and Jeri for answers.

"I'm thinking, I'm thinking," Shaniya said, stressed and pacing.

Suddenly, she had an idea. She opened her mouth, and she sang. She slowly began singing louder and louder.

"Singing?!" shouted Rai. "What is that going to do?!"

"Just sing what I sing," said Shaniya, looking sternly over at the two Bogos.

They all began to sing out the same tune, following Shaniya's direction, and the melody filled the swamp and echoed through the trees. A cool wind blew through the trees, and the swamp began to shake as it did.

The ground shook like a terrible earthquake, rattling Rai, Jeri, Shaniya, Fern, and everything else throughout the swamp. The birds flew out from the trees, and the mud began to bubble up, expelling large amounts of smelly air as the bubbles exploded at the swamp's surface.

"Keep singing!" shouted Shaniya.

They continued to belt out the melody, and as quickly as Malachi and Zeke had sunk into the unforgiving swamp, they rose. As if they were riding an elevator, Malachi emerged from the ground, followed by Zeke, covered in mud and still holding on to each other. They were pushed up and out like the ground was throwing up unsatisfactory food.

Sitting on the swamp's surface, Malachi and Zeke heard cheering from the others. It rang loudly throughout the area. Zeke looked back at them and, with a muddy face and large smile, his shiny white tooth shining among the mud mask, he let out a loud cheer and waved at them.

As the two of them held on to each other, a portion of the ground beneath them also lifted from the swamp. It appeared as if they were sitting atop a pitcher's mound, a large hill that jutted up from the earth.

The ground again began to tremble, and another tiny pitcher's mound rose only a few feet away from the other, this time closer to the spot where Rai stood watching. The smaller hill rose until it popped right up out of the ground. The large ball of swamp was suspended right in front of Rai, floating above the surface.

"What is that?" yelled Jeri, who stood on her tiptoes on the stump, with Fern slipping from her arms like a rag doll.

The sphere that floated in front of Rai then shook side to side, and as the mud was thrown from it, two large, tired eyes opened, looking her straight in the face. They blinked.

"AH!" yelled Rai, frozen in fear.

The mud slipped away, exposing wrinkles on a very old, weathered face. A large, muddy head was supported by a long, thin neck. Once the big eyes gained their vision and clarity, focusing in on Rai, the face let out a loud, deep roar that sent Rai running off and screaming.

"Who's there?" shouted the wrinkled face in a grumpy and tired tone.

"Back here!" shouted Malachi as the face turned around and stretched out its neck, turning to look behind it.

"What are you doing, sitting atop my shell?" it questioned the boy.

Malachi looked down at the hard surface that he and Zeke sat on and, noticing the long neck that connected the face to it, realized he was talking to a humongous, prehistoric turtle.

"Oh, I'm very sorry! We didn't mean any harm!" said Malachi as he stood up and picked Zeke up.

"We're very sorry for disturbing you," he continued, giving his best effort to hide the stuttering nervousness of his voice. "We were just making our way down this path and accidentally stumbled upon you."

The old turtle turned his large body around so that his shell would then butt up against the hard ground where the path had ended. Malachi and Zeke jumped down to join their friends as Jeri and Rai ran up and embraced Zeke. Fern jumped at Malachi's calves, and he picked her up as she licked at his dirty face.

"Did someone call me?" he questioned them.

Shaniya stepped forward, raising her hand in the air.

"It was me. Sorry to disturb you. My friends were in danger, and I wasn't sure what else to do," she said.

"I don't see many outsiders in this area. It's pretty dangerous for little things like you," said the old turtle. "Seems like I was in the right place at the right time. You almost became this swamp's dinner. Be careful. It will swallow you whole."

"Yes, we're very grateful," responded Malachi. "You saved our lives, thank you!"

"Thanks!" grunted Zeke.

"It wasn't me who saved your life. You should thank her!" he said as he tossed his head over toward Shaniya.

"I was sound asleep. You interrupted my nap," snapped the grumpy turtle. "And now I'm kind of hungry," he said, turning to look at Rai. She backed away from him.

"How did you know we were here?" questioned Malachi to the turtle.

"I didn't. I heard the turtle call, and I answered," he replied.

"What's a turtle call?" asked Malachi, turning to look at Shaniya.

"It's a story that the village elders have passed down for many years," she responded. "I heard about it in bedtime stories. I didn't even know if it was real."

"Oh, tell me a story. Please!" begged Jeri.

"Well," said Shaniya, "the story goes that a long time ago, on an island here in Fiji named Kadavu, bad people captured two women. They put them in a small boat and took them out into the ocean. But, while they were out there, a big storm began. Large waves crashed into the boat, and it started to flood."

"Whoa, what happened next?" questioned an intrigued Jeri.

"The women disappeared!" said Shaniya dramatically.

"What? How is that possible?" asked Jeri again, leaning forward.

"They had magically been transformed into giant turtles and sat at the bottom of the boat. The boat began to sink, and to save their own lives, the bad people threw the giant turtles overboard. So, today, the descendants of those turtles continue to respond to the song of the locals, rising to the surface whenever they hear it. And that is what is known as 'turtle calling.'"

"That is so...amazing!" shouted Jeri. "Wow."

"It's true," said the turtle, nodding slowly.

"I'm glad you tried it!" responded Malachi to Shaniya, "or Zeke and I would be gone for good!"

"What're you all doing in this swamp?" he questioned.

"We're looking for the Coral Coast," replied Malachi. "We were told we would find it at the end of this path."

"Oh yes, the Coral Coast!" replied the turtle. "Unfortunately, that coast dried up many years ago."

"Wait, what?!" shouted Rai.

"Really?" asked an alarmed Malachi.

"Nah, I'm just kidding," said the turtle, laughing, in a deep and raspy tone. "What's taking you to the coast?"

"They were told they would find a magic door there to get them home," responded Shaniya.

"Never heard of this magic door before," he said. "But it seems like you've reached the end of your path, kids. There's only a swamp here. No magic, I can assure you."

"Magic doesn't smell like this!" he added with a raspy laugh.

"Ugh," said Jeri, as she rolled her eyes.

"Marina told us we would find the door on the Coral Coast," said Malachi. "Is this the way?"

"Marina? The Spoon Lady, Marina?" asked the turtle, intrigued.

"Yes," responded Malachi.

"I know her! Wow, she's about as old as I am, and I've been lounging around on this island since having to dodge dinosaur mud-wrestling competitions," said the turtle. "How is the old lady?"

"She's odd, that's what she is!" shouted Rai. "And now she has us in a swamp looking for a magical door that is somehow supposed to help us get home, and I doubt it even exists!"

"Patience, kid," said the turtle. "If Marina says there's a way, you better bet there's a way. The problem is, you haven't made it to the Coral Coast yet."

"Are we close?" asked Malachi.

"It's still a decent trek," said the turtle, "but I can help you get there. It will take a lot of time off your trip. A shortcut, if you will."

"That would be great, thank you!" responded Malachi. "So, which way should we go? Is there a better path somewhere?"

"With less mud, preferably," added Rai, wiping at the dirt in her fur.

"Nope, not a path." the turtle replied. "Something even better."

Chapter Seventeen
SETEFANO'S ESCAPE

Malachi, Fern, and the Bogos stood before a giant turtle, offering to help them with their journey to the Coral Coast.

"Well, I can help get you to the sugarcane fields, which will get you close to where you want to go," said the giant turtle, "but you'll have to follow the bends of the swamp."

"We can't walk through this slime!" said a perturbed Rai.

"That is where my services come into play," he said. "I can give you a ride there. It won't hurt to give these ancient legs a stretch."

"How will you give us a ride?" asked Rai. "Up upon your shell?!"

"Exactly," he said. "There is plenty of space for you all."

"I refuse!" exclaimed Rai. "You just want to eat us!"

The giant turtle began to laugh loudly, throwing his head back.

"Oh, no! I don't want to eat you." He chuckled. "You seem too sour!"

Jeri and Zeke ran past her through the mud to jump onto the giant turtle's shell.

"Come on, Rai, it's not that bad," said Malachi as he bent down to offer her a piggyback ride to the turtle.

Rai cautiously jumped on Malachi's back, who pushed through the mud to climb atop the turtle with Fern in his arms. Malachi gave them all a boost up and then pushed himself up. The turtle was larger than any other turtle they had ever seen, and his shell comfortably fit them all.

"Well, aren't you coming?" the turtle asked Shaniya.

"Oh no, this is where I stop. I have to return to the village now," Shaniya responded.

"Come on, it's fun up here!" shouted Jeri.

Shaniya laughed.

"Thanks, Jeri, but this is your journey. I was just here to help. My mother and Marina will be expecting me back soon. It was great to meet all of you!" she said, waving at them.

"Bye!" they all shouted to her.

Malachi waved to Shaniya and picked up Fern so she could see.

Now that they were all aboard and set, the turtle slowly turned his ancient body eastward.

They watched from atop the shell as they got farther from where Shaniya stood on the shore. After a moment, she turned around and headed back through the jungle to home.

"The name is Setefano," said the turtle, turning his head around to look at them.

They introduced themselves, and Malachi told him about their adventure and their homes in Tasmania. The mud was thick, but Setefano pushed his way along the swamp.

"OK, now be quiet as we pass through the remainder of the swamp," he whispered. "Not one of us has left this swamp in years, and I just know Mereani will have something to say about it."

"Mereani?" asked Rai.

"She's a turtle friend. Always telling me to watch out for my health. That we're too old to be acting like children."

"There's more like you?" whispered Malachi.

"This swamp is filled with secrets," whispered Setefano in response. "Here in the swamp, it's nap time, and there's nothing worse than waking a herd of prehistoric, grumpy turtles, I tell ya. Now quiet."

They looked out at the barren swamp as Setefano pushed through it. The large trees draped their vines down into the mud around them, and the swamp occasionally bubbled, releasing a horrible smell. Flies flew around them, and Rai swatted at them in disgust.

A large bubble began to rise from the swamp as they passed. Zeke stuck his finger out, and it popped loudly, letting out a large amount of smelly green gas.

Setefano tensed up at the sound, stopping in his tracks and closing his eyes really hard. He sat there momentarily, waiting, hoping the noise hadn't disturbed anything. After a moment of nothing, he began to move forward again slowly.

"Phew," groaned Setefano.

Suddenly, the surrounding swampland began to bubble and shake.

"Oh no," whispered Setefano. "They're waking up!"

He swam faster, throwing all caution to the wind, as dozens of mounds began to form around them. They rose from the depths as large heads started to pop up from the surface around them. A multitude of grumpy, ancient turtles were waking up and opening their gigantic eyes one by one.

"Hold on!" shouted Setefano as the ground shook them terribly.

The turtles all began to grumble and complain, yelling at Setefano as he passed by quickly.

"Who woke me up?" shouted one of the turtles.

"Is that a human?" shouted another.

"What are the little furry things?"

"I'm starving. Let's eat them!" said a giant turtle, reaching its neck toward them.

Rai screamed as it got closer. The other turtles cackled.

"Setefano! Is that you?" shouted a voice from the distance.

"Can't talk right now, Mereani!" he shouted back.

"Come back here!" the turtle shouted.

Setefano kept swimming as quickly as possible and was soon out of reach of the others. Jeri and Zeke jumped around, waving celebratory goodbyes to the distancing turtles. Rai held tight to the turtle's muddy shell as Malachi held on to Fern and turned to give a wave.

Setefano laughed.

"Woo-hoo!" he shouted. "We made it!"

"That was close!" shouted Malachi.

You could still hear all of the turtles shouting at them from behind.

As they made their way through the mud, the swampy water beneath them began to loosen and clear until a running stream flowed steadily. The stream allowed the ancient turtle to move along faster. The fresh water also gave him a much-needed bath, washing away the mud from his body, which had not taken place for quite some time. The clean bath better exposed his old, wrinkled exterior and large, weathered shell.

Setefano pressed his large face into the stream and filled his mouth with water. Then, turning to look at the group on his back, he sprayed them all with a shower, which further cleaned their fur and skin of the caked-on mud from the swamp. He laughed a huge belly laugh in his raspy voice.

Rai shrieked.

"There, now you're all clean!" Setefano laughed.

They all cheered, except for Rai, and shook the water from their fur.

The large, crowded trees and constricting vines of the forest cleared away. The stream now ran atop the edge of a cliff, and the view was immaculate, as if they stood upon the highest mountain, looking out across the rest of the island. Malachi saw a beautiful landscape of tropical forests, deep valleys, and white-capped shores. The sky was cobalt blue, greatly contrasting with the palms' bright, luscious greenery. Birds, bright in color, flew around them like miniature rainbows with wings. The bird calls were loud and exotic, foreign to their ears. They all stared out at the scene with wide eyes and gaping mouths.

"It's so beautiful!" shouted Jeri as Zeke jumped up and down, clapping.

"Bird!" he grunted, trying to catch one in his clasping hands.

"Whoa!" shouted Malachi as he reached out to grab and pull him back from the edge.

The motion of the stream picked up, and they sailed at a fast, steady pace. They were moving along much faster than they ever would have on foot. The wind blew through Malachi's hair as he noticed that the forest had almost become somewhat nonexistent. As he tried to figure out their current situation, the turtle gave a fair warning.

"You may want to hold on," he said in his deep voice.

"Why is that?" asked a worried Rai.

However, before the question could be answered, the turtle crossed the threshold of an intense decline. The fast stream turned downward, and the vessel's speed escalated immensely. Setefano sped down the side of the mountain, riding the stream like a seasoned bobsled racer. The group held tight to him and one another as the wind blew through their fur.

Despite the forcing wind, Malachi slowly lifted his head, squinted, and pointed out beside them.

"Look, over there!" he shouted, nudging his head to the side.

The Bogos spotted the flying fish that traveled alongside them. The fish jumped from the water and hovered above the surface. Carried along the stream's path, the fish seemed to race to the finish line. Their pectoral fins moved quickly, like the flapping wings of a tiny hummingbird. The bright sun glimmered upon their scales as they gave the travelers personal escorts along the descending waterway.

Ahead of them, the stream ran straight toward a dark tunnel, a cave, at the base of the hill. They all ducked as the giant turtle took them straight down into the dark abyss, starkly contrasting with the bright blue skies and the sunny day outside. The turtle's speed slowed as the ground leveled. They began to float through the dark tunnel slowly.

The eerie, hollow echoes of water dripping throughout the cave and a damp, musky smell were all their senses could make out. It was as dark as a moonless midnight sky, so much so that no living thing could make out the other. The gigantic turtle continued to float on as the group upon his back held tight to one another. The water's current blindly carried them into the dark, mysterious cavern.

Chapter Eighteen

THE TWINKLING CAVE STARS

"I don't like this one bit!" exclaimed a worried Rai as they floated through the cave.

"It's really dark in here," said Malachi as he put his hand to his face. "I can't see anything."

The cave was quiet and echoed only the eerie sounds of water splashing against the rock walls and dripping from the ceiling above to the stream, where they continued to float atop Setefano.

"Look at all the pretty stars!" said Jeri.

Everyone looked up. They could see where little lights began to appear on the cave's ceiling. At first, the lights were difficult to see, as everyone's eyes were not yet adjusted to the dark. The tiny lights covered the ceiling of the dark cavern and twinkled as they watched them. It was a beautiful scene set before them, and it helped ease the darkness's weariness. The sparkling glow got brighter as more and more twinkly lights filled the space above them. The lights excited the furry little creatures, who had become mesmerized by them.

"Look at all of these cave stars!" Jeri shouted. "It's beautiful in here."

"Twinkle, twinkle," grunted Zeke.

"I don't think those are stars," replied Setefano.

He was very old and also very wise.

As they gazed in awe at the ceiling, Jeri noticed the small lights begin to move around them. The little lights zoomed around the cave. The cave stars began to get closer to them, moving around quickly, leaving the ceiling above them. Each little light moved in unison with another, and as they got closer, large, sharp teeth began to shine along with them. Malachi frantically dug in his bag for his flashlight.

Malachi held the flashlight and flicked the switch on, shining the light toward the cave's ceiling. The light gave life to the cave stars, and they became hundreds of black winged creatures with sharp teeth swarming around them. At the sight of them, frightened and shocked, the Bogos panicked and screamed, flailing their hands and bodies around. They eventually dropped to their knees, covering their heads with their arms.

At one point in the alarmed fiasco, a rogue hand knocked into Malachi, and he let go of the flashlight, which splashed into the stream below. He watched the light, which now only illuminated the dark waters, sink until it could be seen no more. It was dark again, but everyone knew of the fanged creatures that swarmed above their heads. Setefano swam as fast as he could. The screeching sounds projected by the creatures made the fur stand up on the Bogos' backs, and Fern crouched and growled toward the ceiling.

After a few long moments, the extreme darkness they had endured began to weaken as rays of the sun passed through tiny cracks in the cave's ceiling. The black winged creatures again became visible as the darkness washed away. They no longer swarmed the room, but hundreds hung upside down from the top of the cave.

"I think they are actually bats," said Malachi, peeking upward from his crouched position on the turtle's shell.

"Fruit bats," laughed Setefano. "Absolutely nothing to be afraid of."

"Vampires—to suck our blood!" shouted Jeri as she jumped at Rai with her fingers at the corner of her mouth, imitating fangs.

Rai gasped.

They all stood up slowly, still cautious toward the unfamiliar new animals.

The room brightened, and they could see the inside of the cave for the first time. The once shadowed, narrow, and moist cave was now brought to life: a vibrant, hidden, underground ecosystem that seemed to grow before their eyes. It was a whole new land filled with bushes of colorful flowers and trees with hanging fruit lined the walls and small banks that they floated by. The hundreds of fruit bats perched, hanging from the limbs and lush bushes, eating the fruits.

The stream grew shallow, and the current pushed the giant turtle onto an embankment, where the water seemed to end. Malachi and the Bogos jumped down from his back onto the cave floor. The grass beneath their feet was all soft and green. Butterflies swarmed around them, their colors mixed with the flowers filling the space. It was hard to imagine that they were still in the same cave that had been so bleak before. Zeke patted Setefano's head and then ran off to pick the luscious fruit that hung low enough for him to reach as the rest of them gave their "thanks" and "goodbyes" to Setefano.

"If you continue straight ahead, through the remainder of the cave, you'll reach the sugarcane fields," the old turtle told them. "Once you are there, you will be very close to the Coral Coast; just continue to move forward."

"Thank you again," said Malachi. "You helped us so much."

"We loooove Setefano!" sang Jeri in a sing-songy voice as she shook her bottom and danced.

The ancient turtle gave a slow, responsive nod to Malachi and the Bogos as he began to back himself off the land and back into the water that had carried him there.

"Good luck," said Setefano, floating in the water. "And Malachi," he shouted while he floated away, his voice echoing back to them. "Remember that, sometimes, the journey is just as important as the destination. Don't forget to be present."

"Presents! I love presents!" Jeri shouted as she bounced away. She ran toward Zeke, laughing all the while.

Malachi smiled and waved to Setefano as he disappeared into the cave's darkness.

As the enormous turtle swam away, he left behind him the wake of the water's current that splashed up onto the bank. Malachi saw his flashlight float up on the shore among the small waves. He reached down, picked it up, and dried it off on his pants.

Jeri and Zeke had run up ahead, along with Fern jumping at their heels, as Rai and Malachi silently walked through the cave.

The cave's beauty was awe-inspiring, as vines ran up the sides and covered the ceilings with green leaves and colorful arrays of flowers and fruits. Big tree trunks burst through the walls and grew as high as the ceiling above would allow them. Although they walked through an underground cavern, a bright blue sky was the only thing missing to prove they were not, in fact, in an open-air field.

"You know," said Malachi, looking over at Rai, "my dad was really great, and I miss him a lot. He always traveled when I was small, and I always wished to travel with him. Nothing scared him, and he was always so brave."

Malachi took a deep breath.

"I want to be like he was," he said, "but I'm not."

"What do you mean, Malachi? You seem very brave to me," responded Rai.

"I couldn't save Jeri and Fern in the river or Zeke in the swamp. I can't even get you to like me," he responded. They were both quiet for a long moment.

"Malachi," said Rai, interrupting the silence as she looked at the boy. "What you did for Zeke back there, helping him out of the mud, was really brave. It made me so worried, and I felt so helpless."

"If it weren't for Setefano getting us out, we would have both sunk," said Malachi. "I didn't do a very good job."

"Not true," responded Rai. "You tried your very best. You even risked your life to help him—to help someone very different than you. You didn't have to do that."

"But he's my friend," said Malachi, now stopping to look at Rai. "Humans can be friends with Bogos, Rai."

Rai didn't respond for a moment but instead looked forward at her friends, who were now chasing the bats while throwing fruit at them.

She turned to look at Malachi.

"The only other human I have met, Crimson Hobart, wasn't really protecting us," she finally responded.

"What do you mean? I thought you said he was?" asked Malachi.

"He said he was protecting us from humans because other humans would hurt us if they found us," she responded, then paused. "But, I felt like he was actually imprisoning us. He wanted us to stay in that shed. I know he didn't want what was best for us. I know it."

"You think so?!" asked Malachi, very intrigued by his new knowledge of the man.

"I didn't tell them," she said, pointing at Zeke and Jeri, who were still running around in front of them in the distance. "I wanted to protect them, and I didn't want them to worry or fear."

"Why didn't you leave?" asked Malachi.

"We had nowhere to go," she said, "and I was afraid of other humans. I had never met any others before. I feared they wouldn't want the best for us, just like Crimson Hobart. So we just stayed there in the shed."

"But what made you so afraid?" asked Malachi.

"One day, a lot of vehicles arrived at the mill. I hid all of us in the shed's rafters and watched through a small crack in the roof. I saw them carrying Crimson Hobart out of the house. He seemed ill. He was shouting, and you could tell he was filled with anger. He pointed at the shed where we sat, terrified, and yelled loudly. The others placed him in a car and took him away, and after that, he never returned. He was gone, and I felt safe again as long as he was gone."

"Until I arrived?" asked Malachi.

"Exactly," she said.

"But I'm happy you did," she added, smiling at him. "Now I've met many new humans and see that a human can actually be a friend."

She gave Malachi a big hug, and he squeezed her back.

"I'm sorry I've treated you so poorly," Rai said. "It was hard to trust someone who looked so much like the man who had imprisoned us. Can we be friends?" she asked, pushing away to look at him.

"Yes, we can be friends. Always!" responded Malachi. "Thank you for giving me a chance, Rai. There are a lot of great humans out there. Don't let one bad one change that."

As they walked forward to catch up with the others, they could hear Zeke and Jeri singing, and they watched as they danced around, lively and carefree. The inside of the cave made for a fun and colorful backdrop. The musical creatures welcomed the screeching sounds of fruit bats into their musical dance number throughout the cave, and Rai ran up and joined them. They laughed and sang as their sounds echoed against the limestone walls.

Together, they embraced the beautiful moment, its colors and happiness. There were smiles and jumps, even joined by Fern, who sniffed a few bats along the way. She did this to each one she encountered until a large, pointy smile frightened her, and she ran away whimpering. She ran to Malachi, who reached down and picked her up, reassuring her that everything was OK, and laughed.

Sooner than they realized, they were at the end of the cave. They stood at the exit looking out over a vast sugarcane field. The sky opened up, and it was bright and blue. They could see large palms out in the distance, past the field, separating the sugarcane field from whatever lay beyond it. The smell of damp, fertile soil filled the clean air.

They were almost there. They could see the coast in the distance.

Chapter Nineteen

GOATS IN A SUGARCANE FIELD

The field of sugarcane was vast and expansive. As they looked down from the cave's ledge, the field resembled a jungle: mangled and mysterious. The crops were bright green and fully grown, some reaching heights of 15 feet tall. They towered high above the Bogos, Malachi, and Fern as they slid down the hill and fell into the dirt below. The ground was moist, and as they walked ahead, they each left a set of muddy tracks behind them. They moved through the maze of closely planted canes as they pushed on. The sun above tried its best to shine through the green canopy of opaque leaves hovering above them.

Giant beetles crawled up the stalks of the plants. Zeke and Jeri collected all they could find, picking them from the plants and holding them in their hands. When their hands were full and overflowing with the crawly insects, they ran after Rai with them. Rai escaped by running through the cane, screaming as she weaved through the crops.

"Stop with the bugs!" she yelled.

"Bugs!" yelled Zeke as he ran after her.

Malachi and Jeri watched and laughed.

Zeke turned and ran back over to them, out of breath, panting as he giggled. The bugs in his hands escaped his grasp as they crawled up his furry arms.

"You can come back, Rai," shouted Malachi. "Zeke promised to stop! Isn't that right?" he asked, looking over at Zeke, both still chuckling under their breath.

"Yes," Zeke sighed.

"Rai, come back," yelled Malachi. "Don't go too far!" But his voice was followed by silence as they all stood, hushed, listening for a response.

"Come on!" he shouted as he started walking in the direction she had gone.

They began to rush in the direction she had last been seen, only to find her path vanished. They called out but heard nothing back from their friend. Malachi grew worried as they all together called out Rai's name.

In the distance, they could hear something, something loud, the cracking of cane, and Zeke yelled and took off running toward the noise.

"Rai, Rai!" he called.

He was only gone for a few moments before his groans and yells grew louder as Zeke turned around and ran back toward them.

"Run, run!" grunted a panicked Zeke as he ran back through the tall sugarcane toward them and then passed them, still running.

Malachi and Jeri exchanged glances, but before they could move, a large herd of goats crashed through the wall of sugarcane, causing an explosion of leaves and stalks. The goats ran past them, following the direction Zeke had gone.

"Zeke!" yelled Jeri.

They both looked down the path of the beaten-down cane, then quickly raced down the pathway to find Rai, shouting her name.

The muddy terrain beneath their feet changed to rocky as they exited the edge of the field, where the broken-down cane had led them. Rock and vines bordered the field like a built wall. In it, they saw an opening to another dark cave.

"Do you think she's in there?" asked Jeri.

"I hope not," responded Malachi.

"I will find her. You go get Zeke!" shouted Jeri, running into the cave without a moment of thought.

"Wait! Jeri, wait!" yelled Malachi as she disappeared into the darkness.

As Malachi walked closer to the cave, Fern growled at his side.

The sound of the racing, bleating group of goats got louder as they came running back by him. With them, Malachi saw Zeke riding atop one of them.

"Yay!" yelled Zeke as he and the goats passed by Malachi.

"Zeke! Jeri just ran inside. She thinks Rai is in there," Malachi said hurriedly, pointing into the dark cavern.

"Uh-oh," responded Zeke, still sitting on the goat.

"Get down from there. We have to go get Rai," said Malachi, reaching out to help Zeke.

Suddenly, out of the cave's dark entrance, a large serpent tail emerged and grabbed Zeke from the goat, pulling him in as quickly as it had appeared. Malachi recognized it instantly: It was the same color and marked with the same unique pattern as the snake that had tried to attack Jeri in the river the day before. It was Kaliya.

"Zeke!" yelled Malachi, running up to the cave entrance. He was gone.

Malachi and Fern stood there, all alone now, as the wind picked up around them and the sky turned gray and ghostly. The warm breeze blew through his hair, and he pushed it from his face. It was oddly quiet now.

Malachi looked down at the ground and saw Zeke's necklace lying beside his shoe. It had been thrown from the creature during the frenzy. He reached down and picked it up, shoving it inside his backpack. He then grabbed Fern, picking her up and cuddling her into his arms and chest.

"It's me and you, girl," he said nervously with a gulp. "We have to go find them."

Together, they walked into the entrance of the cave. It was wet, and the sound of dripping water and the smell of musty air filled the rocky fortress. He took one step at a time as his eyes adjusted to the dark. He grabbed his flashlight from his backpack and clicked it to turn it on, but nothing happened.

"Oh no," he gasped.

He hit it against his hip several times, shaking water from it. With some work, the light bulb flickered inside, and the flashlight turned on. It illuminated nothing but more darkness ahead.

"Hello," he whispered.

"Zeke?" he whispered louder. "Jeri? Rai? Hello?"

He tiptoed through the darkness, and his shoes stumbled upon the rocks. The steep decline of the ground below him made him step cautiously as he navigated the loose stones and large boulders. He could feel himself traveling deeper into the ground, and as the air around him got colder, he shivered. He concentrated on each step to avoid tumbling forward and rolling down into the cave.

He stopped as he looked up and shone the flashlight's light upward. Surrounding him, where there was once only damp rock, were walls of shining jewels—magnificently shiny and robust jewels with tones in every color. The flashlight glimmered through the translucent stones and lit up the space around him. The steep, rocky floor before him had turned to solid gold.

"Patala," he whispered, remembering Shaniya's story. "The underworld."

As he rounded the corner of a large boulder, his flashlight shone brightly against the reflective skin of the large serpent and the walls of jewels surrounding it. He gasped and retreated back to the opposite side of the boulder, breathing heavily.

He bent down and sat Fern on the ground behind the boulder.

"Stay here," he whispered.

He walked back to the edge of the rock and again shone his light, cautiously, over at where the snake had been. He could see its long, thick body coiled up. Its tail was stretched out far, and as he followed along it with the light of his flashlight, he saw his friends imprisoned in the hold of the serpent's tail.

Malachi knew it was up to him to find a way to rescue them. He also knew that he was no match for the giant serpent. How could he get them away from it without it noticing him? If it did catch him, that would surely be the end for them all.

Malachi felt a brush against his leg that made him jump.

"Agh," he gasped. "Go lay down, Fern," he whispered as he brushed at his leg.

However, the feeling continued, and he quickly realized that whatever was behind him was much too large to be Fern.

Malachi turned around quickly, and his flashlight lit up a face that stood level with his. A pair of offset eyes stared right into his as his heart fluttered in fear. It stared back at him, chewing on a branch of the sugarcane from the field.

"Maa," the goat bleated.

The goat from outside, the same one that had carried Zeke, had followed them inside the cave. It now waited with Malachi and Fern behind the rock. Malachi reached out and put his hand on the muzzle of the animal.

"Shh," he whispered as Fern rubbed up against his leg.

He glanced around at the serpent, his trapped friends, and then at the goat. He reached out and grabbed the branch from its mouth, and as he moved the cane, the goat's head and gaze followed.

"You like this?" he whispered, reaching forward and putting the sugarcane before the goat's face.

It took a few steps forward as it tried to reach the sweet sugarcane. Malachi shook it, and the goat got more excited as he did, now prancing with vigor.

Malachi sat his backpack on the ground, unzipped it, and fished to the bottom to find the long-handled spoon necklace Marina had given to Zeke. He pulled it out and used the attached purple string to tie the sugarcane to the end of the spoon. He held out the spoon like a wand and, at the end of it, dangling from the string like bait on a fishing pole, was the sweet piece of cane.

"Come on, girl," he said, bending down to take Fern in his arms. "Just stay in here for a while," he whispered, setting Fern inside the backpack and placing it back on his shoulders. He turned to look back at her as much as he could, and she licked at his face.

"OK, quiet," he said, petting the goat and slowly climbing on its back. Malachi exhaled, expelling some of the fear that had built up in his chest. "We've got this."

He held out the spoon, and the sugarcane dangled before the goat. It moved to bite at it but was unable to reach it. Taking one step forward again, then another, the goat tried to get the cane that hung out of its reach.

They rounded the corner of the large boulder that had been their hiding place, now completely exposed to the serpent. The large snake still slept.

Then, like a cowboy in the rodeo, Malachi kicked the side of the goat, causing it to lunge forward. He steered the goat, still chasing the sugarcane tied to the spoon. They were headed directly toward his friends.

As they approached, Kaliya heard the clogging of the goat's hooves and opened his numerous red eyes as all five heads lifted from the ground. Malachi reached out and grabbed the closest Bogo he could reach. It was Jeri. She clung to Rai, who clung to Zeke, as Malachi pulled all three of them up onto the goat's back. Malachi steered the goat toward the cave's exit and spurred it forward.

Now awake and aware, the serpent reared up and jolted toward them. It chased after them through the rocks and boulders that filled the cave. Malachi kicked at the goat's sides.

"Come on!" he shouted.

The stone behind them crumbled as the serpent ripped through the cave. The goat ran faster, straining under their weight as they held on tightly. They shot out of the cave into what should have been sunlight. Instead, it was storming. The dull gray sky above them spouted down rain as they raced away from the cave. Kaliya darted out of the darkness as well. He slithered behind them as they raced back through the cane field.

"Go, go!" shouted Malachi at the goat.

The goat's speed was no match for the giant serpent, and it began to gain on them, blasting the stalks of cane high in the air as it plowed through them.

"Malachi!" screamed Rai from behind him. "It's very close!"

Rai looked back to see the red eyes of the serpent, only feet away from the back of the goat. It was then that she noticed, in the corner of her eyes, a green light quickly approaching from across the field. Suddenly, the green light smacked into the serpent's side, sending it and the bright light flying into the air. When they fell back to the ground, there were two giant serpents: Kaliya and one that shone the bright green light.

"It's Degei!" Rai shouted. "He's come to save us!"

The goat raced forward, but its riders turned their heads to watch the serpents battle each other.

The goat did not slow down until it had exited the sugarcane field. As it blasted through the final cane stalks, it stopped suddenly, and all five passengers tumbled to the ground. The gray clouds above had gone, and as they exited the tall shadows of the sugarcane, they emerged under a clear Fijian sky.

Malachi and the Bogos stood up, brushing themselves off, and looked out at the vibrant green grass of the pasture they now stood in. They could see more goats in the distance, eating at the grass. Malachi untied the sugarcane branch from the spoon. He draped the spoon and necklace back around Zeke's neck and gave the sugarcane to the goat, who took it and chewed happily.

"Good job," said Malachi. "You deserve this!"

He petted the goat's face, and it turned and galloped toward the others. As he turned around, he saw Bogos running at him. As they approached him, one by one, they all embraced him in their small little arms. The hug was so strong that it knocked Malachi over onto the ground. He laughed.

"Malachi!" grunted Zeke, able to pronounce the boy's name for the first time.

They let go of each other and, looking across the grassy pasture, realized they could see the ocean. The palm trees that stood above them, swaying in the breeze, were the same trees they had seen from a distance. They were separated from the beach by only a small sandy dune of bushes and grass. Beyond it, they could see the majestic turquoise of the ocean, clear and glassy in the sunlight.

They were almost home.

Chapter Twenty
FOLLOW THOSE EELS

"We made it!" shouted Malachi, looking down to Fern, who replied with a twirl and a wagging tail.

The Bogos ran through the flowered dune to the white sandy beach as he and Fern ran after them. The Bogos chased one another around the beach, laughing and tumbling through the sand. Malachi stopped and stood back, watching his newly made friends. He had experienced so much in the past few days and realized now that the company he had kept had made his adventure so enjoyable. He missed home, especially Granny Annie, but he knew he would also miss his new friends and the fun they were having when—and if—he finally made it back to the mill.

"Did we make it? Is this the Coral Coast?" shouted Jeri.

"Let's hope so!" he responded.

A part of him was not ready to end this adventure. He looked around, lifted his hand, and grabbed onto his father's hat. He thought of his parents and how he missed his family. Watching the Bogos play, he wondered what his parents would have thought of his new friends. He knew they were not your regular neighborhood playmates, but he also knew his parents would have loved them just the same. They would have found the Bogos funny, just like he did. These crazy, unique creatures had become very special to him, and he couldn't help but think of them as his newly found family.

He wiped the tears from his eyes, letting go of the hat atop his head, and walked out onto the beach with them.

"Tag, you're it!" yelled Jeri as she zoomed past Zeke, smacking him on the back so hard he almost tumbled over.

"Ow!" he grunted, regaining his balance. He took off after her, white sand thrown from the bottom of their little running feet.

Malachi walked to the ocean's edge, removed his shoes, and rolled his pants legs up. He waded out, not far from the shore, and reached into the water, where a bright blue starfish sparkled in the sand. He held it under the surface, turning it over and observing its beauty. It was brighter than any other starfish he had ever seen, not that he had seen that many in real life anyway. As he held it in his hand, he suddenly caught a glimpse of something glittery swim quickly past him. He dropped the starfish and scurried back through the water to the shore.

"What was that?" he shouted.

It was then that he looked up and noticed the colors of the sky in the distance.

"The sun!" he shouted at the Bogos. "It's turning the sky orange! It's almost dusk."

"What should we do?" asked Rai.

"We don't have much time. We have to find that shoal," Malachi responded as he looked in both directions down the beach's coast.

"There's nothing here," said Jeri, panting and breathless from running around with Zeke.

Again, from the corner of his eyes, Malachi saw the movement in the water. He turned his head to see something very colorful swim past him. It swam just a bit deeper out in the water.

"Did anyone else see that?" he asked.

Before Malachi could complete his sentence, Jeri began to run. He was not the only one to see the bright streak beneath the surface. Jeri ran along the shore in the direction it had gone.

"It went this way!" she shouted, motioning for the others to follow.

"We don't have time," shouted Malachi. "We are going to miss our chance to cross over!"

"Come on!" she shouted back.

She ran along the beach as the rest raced to catch up. They rounded the sharp bend of the shore, and through the maze of palm trunks that towered above them, they saw the outline of a rocky islet set out from the ocean's shore.

"That's it!" Jeri shouted.

"We don't know that!" Malachi responded, still running. "Marina said there are many of them, like five hundred!"

"It's there!" responded Jeri, pointing at the mysterious swimming glimmer they had chased down the shore.

"Where's the shoal? We need the shoal!" Rai shouted at the glimmer, which then took off again, following the bends of the shore.

They all chased behind it and closed in on the rocky islet.

"It's not the right one!" said Malachi.

"How do you know that?" questioned Jeri.

Both of them were out of breath from running in the sand.

"There is no way to cross over to that. We must keep looking for one with a sand bridge," he responded.

They kept running behind the swimming streak of light and noticed a break in the water not far ahead, which caused small whitecaps in the water's current. They saw the sandbank that jutted out from the shore as they got closer. It went straight to the islet.

"Look!" shouted Jeri, pointing. "It's the one!"

"Jeri, you found it!" shouted Malachi.

The tide had already begun to rise beneath the orange sun quickly setting behind the horizon.

"We have to go now! Go, go!" shouted Malachi, who was waving them on.

Jeri ran out on the narrow strip of the sand bridge as Malachi stayed behind to wait for his friends. Zeke and Fern approached him quickly and ran to catch up with Jeri, who was running toward the islet.

Malachi waited at the water's edge for Rai to catch up. She was struggling to keep up her pace. The sandbank continued to shrink as it succumbed to the rising tide.

"Keep running!" yelled Malachi to Jeri and Zeke, who were now almost to the rocks in the distance.

Behind them, the water filled the bridge passageway as the waves nipped at their ankles.

"Come on, Rai!" he shouted, who struggled to catch her breath. She was slowing down.

Malachi ran back down the coast toward her as the water rushed over the shoal. Jeri, Zeke, and Fern stood abandoned on the rocks in the distance. A shallow layer of water now completely covered the sand bridge.

Malachi approached Rai, who stood bent over.

"I've got you!" he said, bending down and picking her up. He ran them both back to where the bridge had once been.

"Get on my shoulders," he told her.

As she climbed atop the boy's shoulders, he walked out into the water, which was now ankle-deep. As he quickly made his way across, the water continued to get deeper. His knees, his waist, his stomach, and then his chest submerged in the ocean. He slowed drastically as he struggled to get a foothold with each step, the current now trying to sweep him under. His face barely stayed above the ocean's surface as Rai sat on his shoulders, now with wet fur.

"Ahh!" he yelled as he grimaced and struggled, trying to slowly and steadily take steps forward against the ocean's current.

"Come on, Malachi!" yelled Jeri in the distance.

"Hurry!" yelled Zeke, who was jumping up and down.

Rai held tightly to Malachi.

The rising tide crashed against his face and made it hard to breathe. He gasped for air when he could. With all that he had, he tried to remain standing as he held on to Rai. But, with all that he gave, he was no match for the roaring ocean.

His feet were swept from under him.

Malachi and Rai floated away from the sand bridge. Malachi paddled his legs as hard as he could as he held on to Rai. She clung to one of his arms as he kicked his legs vigorously in the depths of the water. Waves washed over them, and Malachi, with one arm free, paddled and kicked to no avail. The current continued to wash them out to sea, further away from the islet where the others stood, panicked.

Malachi fought against the swells of the ocean, splashing water and flailing. As he tried his hardest to stay afloat and paddle against the water's rage, all while holding on to Rai, he heard Granny Annie's voice.

"That's a doggy paddle. It'll get you nowhere," said Granny Annie to him as he splashed and kicked as hard as he could to stay afloat.

"Rotary strokes!" she said. "One arm after the other, kick and kick."

In his memory, Malachi stretched out his arm in front of him, and as it dipped back below the surface, he pushed the water behind him. Then, he did the same with the other arm. He kicked his feet.

He was doing it. He was swimming.

"Exactly! That's it!" said Granny Annie.

"Hold on to my shoulders!" said Malachi to Rai.

Rai repositioned herself on his back, holding on to his neck and shoulders.

"One arm after the other," he said aloud to himself. And as he did, he began his rotary strokes, with each arm stroke pushing water behind him as he kicked. One long stroke of the arm after another, Malachi got closer to the rocks in the distance.

Ahead of him, the glow of the glimmering water creature caught his eye. As he got closer, it zoomed toward him and started circling Malachi and Rai in the water. The water grew lighter, reflecting the creature's colors, which Malachi still couldn't make out. Suddenly, it split into two different creatures, now circling them in opposite directions, weaving in and out of each other.

Malachi could see them now. The creatures in the water were eels. They weren't plain green eels, however. These eels that swam around him were vibrant and striped with shades of red and orange and hints of purple under the setting sun's reflection. They were very long, and their patterns were intricate and unique. However, the most unusual aspect of these eels was that they glowed.

The eels darted back toward the islet and hovered in the water, right next to the rocks, until Malachi and Rai reached the shore. As he reached out, grabbing the rock with the last of the energy he could muster, Malachi pulled himself and Rai up onto the solid ground. With a splash, the eels jetted off again out into the ocean.

Malachi pushed Rai ahead of him as they climbed up on the ledge. Zeke, Jeri, and Fern peered over at them and cheered from the opposite side. The water continued to splash against the rocks, constantly washing over them as they climbed up to higher ground.

Jeri reached out her hand to them and pulled Rai up to her. They then both reached down, helping Malachi up as well.

"I'm so glad you made it!" shouted Jeri.

"Did you find the Wandering Door?" questioned a soaked and exhausted Malachi. He panted and wiped his wet, shaggy hair from his eyes.

"There's nothing here, Malachi," responded Jeri. "It's just rocks."

"No," exclaimed Malachi. "It has to be here! There has to be a door!"

"Maybe Marina was wrong," said Rai, breathing heavily.

"I don't know, Malachi," added Jeri, "but it's not here."

Chapter Twenty-One
THE WANDERING DOOR

They all stood atop the rocky islet, wet and tired, surrounded by stone made dark by the splashing of the rising tide. The ocean mist sprayed constantly, crashing over rocks and filling in a shallow pool in the center of the islet. The sun flickered on the horizon, casting an array of shadows in the dark orange haze of sunset.

They sat down on the wet stone, washed smooth by the continuous rushing waves of the ocean, at the edge of the small pool. The bottom was sandy and speckled with small rocks and broken shells.

"What should we do now?" asked Malachi. "There's nowhere else to go, and we were just chasing eels."

"Maybe that Spoon Lady really was crazy," said Rai. "We have probably come all this way for nothing. We'll just be stranded on this island forever!"

"We will have to wait until the morning, when the tide lowers and the bridge reappears, to return to the shore," replied Malachi.

"And sleep, here?" Rai gawked in disgust.

"There has to be something else," said Jeri, "something we are missing."

As they sat in a circle, their toes hanging down into the pool of water, they looked around for any signs that may lead them to their next move. Suddenly, a huge wave crashed against the islet. The two glowing eels splashed over the rocks and into the pool of water. Their bright light shone from the water, illuminating their feet and faces.

As the eels began to swim circles in the water, the sand and pebbles at the bottom washed around and moved. With the light of their glow, Malachi looked down in the water. As the sand washed away, it exposed the floor of the pool.

"Everyone, look!" shouted Malachi, reaching down into the pool and brushing away more sand and pebbles with his hand.

The base of the pool was not rock but wood.

"It's the door!" he shouted, brushing harder at the sand.

Rai, Jeri, Zeke, and even Fern helped Malachi, and soon, all of the sand was brushed to the side. When it had all cleared, they saw the huge, arched wooden door beneath the shallow water. The eels continued to swim. They all sat there, perplexed. The arched wooden door had no handles, no keyholes, nothing.

"There's no way to open it," said Rai. "There isn't a space for a key either."

"A key we don't even have," responded Malachi. "Jeri, let's check out the yellow book."

She presented the yellow book to him, and as he opened it, flipping through blank pages, he realized there was nothing new. There was no new knowledge for them to learn from except the pages they had already read. He skimmed them closely but found nothing that could help them now.

"What good is this thing? There's nothing here!" he shouted in frustration.

He threw the book down on the rocky surface, and as the ocean breeze whirled past them, the pages of the book began to flip with force. The yellow book, on its own, turned to the next blank page in the book. He watched as the once-empty page began to fill with words. Like a typewriter filling a page, the lines appeared one by one.

He picked up the book and began to read it aloud.

THE TRAVELER'S KEY

THE TRAVELER'S KEY EXISTS TO ASSIST TRAVELERS AS THEY FULFILL THEIR DESTINY. IT IS WITH THIS KEY, AND THIS KEY ALONE, THAT A HUMAN CAN ACCESS THE

WANDERING DOOR. LIKE ITS CREATOR, THE KEEPER OF LIGHT, THE TRAVELER'S KEY CAN BE TRICKY IN ITS APPEARANCE, OFTEN PRESENTING ITSELF IN MANY FORMS AND INCARNATIONS.

"But we don't have a key!" said Rai.

"She wouldn't have sent us here to be stranded," Malachi said.

"How do you know?" asked Rai. "Then where is it?"

"I don't know," he huffed. "There isn't even a keyhole in the door anyways."

"Think. Think. What did Marina say?" Jeri muttered as she paced the rock.

"Spoon," said Zeke.

"Yes, she has lots of spoons," responded Jeri.

"Spoon!" he exclaimed excitedly, now waving the spoon Marina had given him, which hung on the string around his neck.

"Yes, Zeke, she gave you one of her spoons," said Rai.

"Yes, yes, spoon!" Zeke continued to grunt with animated jumps and gestures.

"Zeke, she was really nice to give you that spoon," said Jeri, smiling and patting him on the head, "but that still doesn't mean she isn't also loony!"

Zeke shook his head aggressively and, standing up, walked to the edge of the shallow water where the eels continued to swim. He glared down at the pool and stood there frozen for a few seconds. He looked back at the group, down at his spoon, and then back at his reflection in the water.

"Spooon," he said once more, drawing out the syllable. Then, closing his eyes, he dipped the spoon into the puddle, stirring it around as he had done to the pots in the village.

He held it like he was a sorcerer whirling his magic wand around. He opened one eye at a time, gazing into the water and down at the spoon, hoping for something magical to happen.

They all stood up, staring into the water.

"Spoon," he said again, this time in a low, saddened voice, as he stepped away from the pool, shoulders and head drooped.

Nothing.

He sat down on the rock, dropping the spoon beside him. With that, everyone else seemed to also lose hope, and one by one, they sat down next to Zeke, collapsing onto the rock.

"It's just a spoon, ole buddy!" said Jeri, scooting over to her friend and giving him a big squeeze. "I guess it was worth a try," she said, smiling and winking at Zeke.

• • • • • • • • • •

MEANWHILE, BACK AT THE VILLAGE, Marina saw a light shining brightly from the large black pot full of purple goo outside. She stepped out of her front door, strolled over to the pot, and stirred the contents inside with the large wooden spoon in her hand. A bright purple glow shone about her face, and she looked down inside and began to speak.

"It wasn't a bad try either!" shouted a voice from the glow of the shallow pool.

"It's Marina!" shouted Jeri.

"You're onto something there, Zeke!" said Marina as she continued to speak to them from the water.

"Where are you?" questioned Rai. Marina laughed.

"Down here!" she responded.

Looking down in the water, they could see Marina's reflection, which had turned a dark plum shade of purple.

"Shaniya told me about Setefano," said Marina. "I'm glad you're all OK. It's been quite the journey, hasn't it?"

"Oh yes," responded Rai. "We only almost died a few times."

"Well, how about we get you all home then!" added Marina. The eels continued to swim in circles inside the shallow pool. "And, Zeke, I see you've discovered the secret Traveler's Key," she said.

"That's the Traveler's Key?" questioned Malachi, pointing at the spoon in Zeke's hand.

"Yep, I've had that spoon sitting around for quite some time," she responded. "Just waiting for you, Malachi. Don't let its looks fool you. This key has great power and shows itself in many different forms. The important part is that you use it for the good of humanity and in fulfilling your purpose and the destiny of these Bogos, who are now a part of you."

Malachi and the Bogos looked at one another, then back down to Marina's reflection in the purple water.

"You have all proven that you have what it takes for the journey that lies ahead of you," Marina continued.

"Jeri, you have the gift of immeasurable joy and enduring patience. Your smile energizes and brings hope when hope may feel lost. Your fur, multicolored and bright, is symbolic of the radiant colors that shine through you. Be proud of the light that you carry.

"Zeke, you embody the desirable trait of curiosity for the unknown. You are excited about the adventure and long to know more about your world and others. Your voice may not be audible, but your love is, and your actions speak grander than any words could.

"Rai, you stand steadfast to your convictions. You are responsible, and you take care of your friends. You find answers and work to keep the pack together. In your pursuit of caution, always give room for adventure as well.

"And Malachi," she said, smiling. "You, my friend, are a leader. You push through, even in the darkest of times, to find the light. You never leave anyone behind, risking your own life for others. You empathize with the weak and needy, and you support your team.

"The four of you will help one another fulfill the destiny set upon each of your lives. You each have something to offer, and none can do it alone. You must learn to understand and be forgiving of one another, trust one another, and guard one another. Although this first journey, a test of your endurance, may soon be over, your lifelong adventure together is just beginning.

"And, of course, what would a great leader be without his trusty sidekick?" laughed Marina, looking over at Fern.

"Our lifelong journey?" questioned Malachi.

"That's right," she said matter-of-factly. "Malachi, you are a chosen Traveler."

"I can't be a Traveler. I still don't understand any of this," responded Malachi.

"You will learn, Malachi. Your first test is complete, and you've passed so easily. This is your destiny, and for this, you exist," responded Marina. "The Traveler is not from one place, but many. Hence the name. You will spend your life exploring the world, its people, and rich cultures and bringing hope to those who need it most."

Malachi looked at the spoon in his hand, and as he did, it began to shift into a long and narrow skeleton key. As quickly as it changed, it shifted back into the spoon.

"But how do I use it? Where does it go?" he asked, but Marina had already faded out of sight.

Fern sniffed toward the puddle of water, lifting her nose in the air. She cautiously walked back over, now with a heavier growl.

"What is it, girl?" asked Malachi.

The eels still swam in the same circles as before.

"Spoon!" yelled Zeke, jumping up and laughing.

"What does this mean?" asked Jeri, with a confused glance at Malachi.

"I have no idea," he responded.

And just like before, he put the spoon down into the water.

Nothing happened.

They all stood there.

"Remember what she said," said Malachi. "You each have something to offer, and no one can do it alone."

"Yes, I remember. It was an entire moment," responded Rai.

"Right. So that means it was important," Malachi added. "We have to do this together. Everyone should come in close. Make sure everyone is touching."

They all huddled together, taking one another's hand into their own. And as they did, Malachi put the key into the water. With a loud crack, the large wooden door flung open, exposing a dark, black abyss under the water's surface.

"We did it!" shouted Jeri as everyone celebrated.

"Jump!" said Zeke, smiling and motioning toward the water. "Jump!"

"You cannot jump in there!" said Rai, looking at the others, who all gave her an unsure stare.

"Well, I am definitely not jumping!" she added. "There's nowhere to go, and there are eels in there."

"It's a portal, Rai," said Jeri. "I think it's the only way."

Before she could finish her sentence, an excited Zeke took off running, and with a cannonball jump, he splashed down into the pool, completely disappearing into the darkness. The rest of the group stepped closer to the pool and looked for Zeke but could not see anything of their friend.

"Here it goes," said Jeri as she tiptoed to the edge, turned to wave goodbye, and fell backward into the water, holding her nose.

Jeri immediately disappeared.

"I won't do it," said an adamant Rai as she crossed her arms and stood her ground with a stomp.

Malachi bent down, and Fern jumped into his arms. He then turned to Rai.

"Come on, we will go together," he said as he reached out to grab her hand, which she then grabbed back.

Malachi tugged gently on Rai's hand, and she smiled at him and followed him over to the edge. They peered into the shallow water, realizing that two of their friends had already disappeared completely. Malachi, reassuringly, looked over to Rai.

"When I say three, we will jump," he said.

She looked back at him nervously.

"Where will we go?" she asked him. "I can't just jump and not know where I am going."

"I'll tell you what my mom used to tell me," he responded and paused. "Sometimes, the best adventures are the unknown ones."

Rai nervously looked up at Malachi and nodded.

"OK," she said, "here goes nothing!"

Malachi then began to count.

"One...two...three!" Together, they jumped into the pool of glowing water.

Once submerged, Malachi opened his eyes to look around the small pool. However, as he did, he noticed a deep, lively reef surrounding him. Looking around, he saw a full community of plants and sea life, making their home upon colorful shelves of coral, waving in the current. Bright fish, blue, yellow, and orange, swam in circles and after one another. There was coral and urchins, slugs, and seagrass—and it had all somehow found its way down into what seemed to be a shallow pool of water.

How is this possible? he thought.

He spotted the two eels, who now swam in circles around him. Floating nearby were his friends. He saw Zeke waving at him and Jeri swimming after a tiny rainbow fish.

Rai was balled up, trying to escape anything swimming close to her. They slowly sank farther down in the water, and the light and colors all began to darken as they plunged deeper and deeper into the pool.

One by one, his friends that had jumped before him sank out of sight. It was so dark in the deep shadows that he could see nothing more than a small round light up above him. The small glimmer of the sun above gave the only illumination to the depths until it, too, disappeared.

The water was dark, and nothing could be seen. Malachi began to panic. He reached for Fern but felt nothing. He flailed his arms as he attempted to swim upward. Faster and faster, he stroked at the water above him, but he could feel himself sinking. He tried to yell but heard nothing. He eventually gave up and closed his eyes.

Chapter Twenty-Two
TURNING THE PAGE

Malachi sat in the darkness. He could hear, in the distance, a familiar sound. The low growl and prancing of feet sounded like it was getting closer. It was Fern. He could tell from the rhythm of her prance. He reached out to grab her and opened his eyes. It was still dark. Very dark. Malachi took in a deep gasp of air. He was on his back, lying on a hard surface. He listened to Fern's growl and blinked his eyes; they adjusted to focus in the dark.

Malachi continued to breathe heavily. It smelled musty and dry. He sniffed the air again and smelled dirt and hay. He felt beneath him; it was a wooden floor. There were crates and barrels around him, and light shone in through small cracks and slivers in the walls. His eyes were now close to being fully adjusted, and he could see Fern standing beside him. He recognized the room; it was the shed at the mill, where he had initially found the Bogos.

He sat up and looked on the floor next to him. Lying beside him, opened up, was his father's journal. He picked up the journal and walked toward the door. He opened the rusty wooden door, letting more light flood the dark room as he stepped outside.

He looked down at the book. It was still open, and he scanned the page full of text, photos, and drawings. As he looked closer, he noticed that everything seemed incredibly familiar.

He brought the journal close to his face.

There was a photo of a mountain range taped to the page.

"The locals call this mountain range 'The Sleeping Giant,'" he read out loud. He traced the words with his finger. It was his father's handwriting.

He then glanced at the next page, listing plants and animals, including giant palms, flying fish, and fruit bats. There was also a photo of his father standing next to a woman.

The village's local doctor, Marina, read the handwritten caption following the photo.

The next page held another taped photo. A village girl stood at the shore, where many sea turtles popped up from the water's surface.

The ancient tradition of turtle calling, read the caption.

Malachi's heart raced, and he dropped the book.

"Jeri, Zeke, Rai!" he shouted, frantically taking his attention from the page.

He ran back inside and looked around the shed, throwing old sacks and knocking over barrels. He yelled for his friends, running back outside. It was evening, and the sun would be setting soon. He once more called for his friends, but there was no response. He picked up Fern in one hand and the book with the other. He pulled the open book closer to his face, scanning its page. He looked at Fern, who licked his face, and then at the old mill house. It looked the same as he had left it. He looked back at the empty shed.

His eyes began to water. Where were they?

He walked across the lawn of the mill, passing the stream and waterwheel where he and Fern had played days before, and then out of the iron gate, giving one last glance behind him.

He and Fern went back to Granny Annie's house through the woods. When he arrived home, it was almost completely dark outside. He walked in, and Granny Annie and Oliver stood in the kitchen. She turned from the stove and her conversation with Oliver, walked over, and gave Malachi a big hug.

"I was wondering if you were going to make it back in time for dinner!" she said. "It's ready, so you can go wash up."

Malachi stood there, still trying to understand.

"Haven't you missed me?" Malachi asked.

"I surely have," said Granny Annie. "I miss you every day when you go exploring."

"How long have I been gone?" he asked determinedly.

"Well, I'm unsure of the exact time you left this morning," she said. "You ran out of here pretty quickly."

"Only one day?" he asked, amazed at her calmness.

"Almost one entire day!" she said, chuckling. "I was wondering if you would make it home this evening. It's already dark out. Are you alright, Malachi?"

"I think so," he said hesitantly, turning and walking to his room.

Oliver looked at Granny Annie, both of them shrugging.

Malachi placed his father's journal on the bed and looked at it momentarily. He thought back to the friends he had met. He missed them.

Had he made it all up? Surely not.

He turned and sat on the bed next to the book. As he did, something in his back pocket poked him.

"Oww!" he groaned.

He slowly reached behind him and pulled a spoon from his pocket: Zeke's spoon, the Traveler's Key. He stared at it, slowly removing his hat to scratch his head. Immediately, he realized what he had done. He still wore his father's hat when he jumped into the pool. He looked at the two objects in his hands and quickly turned, gasping, to look at the book.

Granny Annie stood at the door, watching, unbeknownst to him. He opened the book to the first page, which he had stared at many times before. It was the picture of his parents in snowsuits. He flipped to the next page.

"Fiji," he read. His father had written it as a title across the top of the page. Below it were the pictures of Marina and the turtle call.

He looked over the page once more, remembering his journey. Granny Annie smiled as she watched Malachi from the doorway. Malachi then took a deep breath as he again turned the page of his father's journal.

THE END

(OR, PERHAPS, JUST THE BEGINNING)

ACKNOWLEDGMENTS

As Setefano reminds us in this story, it is not about the destination but the journey. I wholeheartedly believe that. Over 10+ years of writing the world and characters of *The Wandering Adventures at Hobart Mill*, I have had so many moments, locations, and people who have inspired aspects of this novel. I couldn't possibly begin to name them all. But writing this book has pushed me to put myself in situations that have stretched my spirit, expanded my mind, and brought me joy. It has been a long, fulfilling journey.

THANKS TO MY HUSBAND, ERIK. Thank you for always supporting my dreams, championing my goals, and loving me when I feel unlovable. Thank you for being my forever plus one, travel buddy, pandemic partner, fellow dreamer, and true love. Look, we dreamt it, and we did it. We published a book!

THANKS TO MY DEAR FRIEND AND EDITOR, ALLISON. From bonding over being the outcasts of a writing group, to becoming great friends, to being my marriage witness and becoming a part of my family and "Auntie Allison" to my pets, to being my editor and creative collaborator, you make my life, and this book, better!

THANKS TO MY MOM. Since I was a boy, you have always encouraged my creativity and have given me the space to explore it. You have had my back through life's ups and downs, always gave all you could to allow me opportunities for a fulfilling life, and never failed to ask every writer's favorite question, "Is the book finished yet?"

THANKS TO MY MA. You are my sunshine. I never thought I'd get you to visit New York City, but I can mark that off my bucket list now. I consider myself blessed to have a grandmother who always encourages, supports, and protects me. Thanks for always being that cornerstone of the family and always stepping up to that plate 110%.

THANKS TO MY (CHOSEN) FAMILY AND FRIENDS. You all know who you are. Whether you were there as a sounding board, a collaborator, an encourager, a supporter, an inspiration, or a reader, my sincere thanks and gratitude cannot be properly expressed in this one paragraph. It takes a village, truly.

(Special shout-out to Cody Cobb, Dee Dillingham, Ryan Fender, Kris Fuchs, Kristina Wrenn Gaskins, Patrick Godwin, Jessica Butler Hill, Donna Kearney, Quzon McCarthy, Kristofer Pistillo, Vicki Coker Powers, and Stephanie Butler Scott.)

THANKS TO MY ILLUSTRATOR, RICHARD MICHAEL GOMEZ. You visually brought these characters to life in such a fun and vivid way. Thanks for all the hard work. The cover turned out great!

THANKS TO SYDNEY, AUSTRALIA; CHARLESTON, SOUTH CAROLINA; AND NEW YORK, NEW YORK. I have called each of you home during the writing process of this book. You have each added a unique energy and feel to this story and have built me into the writer I am today.

THANKS TO FIJI. My time spent on your beautiful island inspired me enough to write this story. I love and appreciate your rich culture, stories, and people. Thank you for sharing them with me.

THANKS TO YOU, THE READER. I'm thrilled that you have decided to go on this adventure with me. This book would be nothing if you had not decided to pick it up and explore the pages within.

ABOUT THE AUTHOR

DUSTIN C. KINARD was born and raised in the Low-country of South Carolina, on the outskirts of Charleston. He has always loved English and the arts and started his early career as his high school's yearbook editor, designer, and journalist. After graduating from an international leadership college, he worked as a non-denominational associate pastor, where he wrote and developed children's curriculum and plays. During this time, he began creating some of the characters still used in his writing today.

Dustin has lived abroad in Sydney, Australia, and has traveled to places like India, Colombia, and Bali for months. He often travels and explores the world, collecting art and gathering stories for himself and his readers. He loves all forms of storytelling, including a particular interest in puppetry. Travel remains his greatest muse.

As a traveler, Dustin enjoys immersing himself in culture, often off the beaten path, where he stays in homes with local families, joins in on religious ceremonies and experiences, and feasts on the traditional cuisine around a dinner table. A common theme in his writing is that he draws influence from native lore, spirituality, mythology, tall tales, and his favorite artists and stories.

Dustin resides in New York City with his husband, Erik; their cats, Brea and Emmet; and their golden retriever, Cub. He spends his days at the dog park, enjoying Broadway shows, and catching his favorite musicians' concerts—when he's not traveling the world.

DUSTINCKINARD.COM
INSTAGRAM: DUSTINCKINARD

* 9 7 9 8 9 8 9 8 6 3 0 0 6 *